A Brave [Knight]
Does Battle

"**I**n the name of Dulcinea, prepare for my lance!" Don Quixote yelled as Rozinante thundered along at top speed. An energy he had never felt before ran through Don Quixote's body. He aimed his lance at his opponent's chest. It hit the Knight of the Mirrors squarely and sent him flying off his horse.

"I don't believe it!" Sancho yelled, climbing down the tree as fast as he could. He ran over to stand beside Don Quixote at the fallen knight's side.

"Is he dead?" Sancho asked.

WISHBONE™ Classics

Don Quixote

by Miguel de Cervantes

retold by Michael Burgan

Interior illustrations by Hokanson/Cichetti

Wishbone illustrations by Kathryn Yingling

HarperPaperbacks

A Division of HarperCollins*Publishers*

HarperPaperbacks *A Division of* HarperCollins*Publishers*
10 East 53rd Street, New York, N.Y. 10022

Copyright ©1996 Big Feats! Entertainment
All rights reserved. No part of this book may be used or reproduced in any manner whatsoever without written permission of the publisher, except in the case of brief quotations embodied in critical articles and reviews.
For information address HarperCollins*Publishers*,
10 East 53rd Street, New York, N.Y. 10022.

Cover photographs by Carol Kaelson

A Creative Media Applications Production
Art Direction by Fabia Wargin Design
Project Management by Ellen Weiss
Edited by Joanne Mattern

First printing: April 1996

Printed in the United States of America

HarperPaperbacks and colophon are trademarks of
HarperCollins*Publishers*
WISHBONE is a trademark and service mark of
Big Feats! Entertainment

❖ 10 9 8 7 6 5 4 3 2 1

Introduction

Sancho Panza

All set to enter a world of action, adventure, drama, and laughs? Then come along with me, **Wishbone**. You may have seen me on my TV show. Often I am the main character and sometimes I am the sidekick, but I'm always right in the middle of a thrilling story. Now, I'm going to be your guide as we explore one of the world's greatest books — DON QUIXOTE. Together we'll meet a lot of interesting characters and discover places we've never been! I guarantee lots of surprises too! So find a nice comfy chair, and get ready to read with **Wishbone**.

Table of Contents

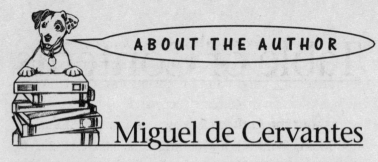

Miguel de Cervantes

Let me introduce you to Miguel de Cervantes Saavedra. (His friends—like me—call him Cervantes.) Cervantes had a big imagination, and he wrote the exciting story of Don Quixote and his sidekick, Sancho Panza. Like the character he created, Cervantes lived a life full of adventure.

Cervantes was born in the city of Alcala de Henares in Spain in 1547. His father was a nobleman, but his family was very poor.

By the age of 16, as a student in Seville, Spain, Cervantes was already a writer. He published his first work, a poem honoring the Queen of Spain, a few years later.

Cervantes was also a brave soldier. When he was 23, he fought in the famous sea battle of Lepanto in Greece. Although badly injured, he continued to serve as a soldier and fight in other battles.

After one battle off the coast of France, Cervantes was taken prisoner. He spent five long years as a slave. When he was finally freed, he returned to Spain.

Cervantes was always writing. He wrote plays, poems, and novels. He published his first novel, *Galatea*, in 1585. Sadly, Cervantes struggled as a writer and had to work at other jobs to earn money.

In 1605, Cervantes published his masterpiece, the great novel of a knight and his adventures, *Don Quixote*. The book was an immediate success!

At the time Cervantes wrote *Don Quixote*, stories of knights, chivalry, and romance were extremely popular in Spain. However, there had not been an actual knight in Spain for a long, long time. Readers loved these books about knights, but Cervantes thought they were silly. He wrote *Don Quixote* as a parody of the books. (A parody is a work that makes fun of something by imitating it.) In *Don Quixote*, Cervantes makes fun of books about knights through the character of Don Quixote. Through *Don Quixote*, Cervantes shows what would happen if someone really lived as the characters did in these popular books.

People in Spain loved the book *Don Quixote*. They especially loved the character of the heroic knight with his enthusiastic spirit and his lively imagination.

The book was so popular that another writer became jealous. He wrote a book about Don Quixote and insulted Cervantes throughout the book. Cervantes quickly wrote his own sequel to *Don Quixote*, so readers would know what really happened to the characters of Don Quixote and Sancho Panza.

On April 23, 1616, a year after he published the second part of *Don Quixote*, Cervantes died while traveling across Spain. He is still considered one of the world's greatest authors.

Alonso Quixana (ah-LON-so kee-AHN-nah)—A middle-aged farmer who loves to read books about knights and their adventures.

Don Quixote (DON kee-HOE-tay)—The name Alonso Quixana takes when he begins his knightly adventures.

Sancho Panza (SAHN-cho PAHN-zah)—Don Quixote's neighbor, who becomes his squire and accompanies him on his adventures.

Rozinante (roz-in-AHN-tay)—Don Quixote's horse.

Aldonza (all-DON-za)—The girl Don Quixote loves.

Dulcinea (dool-sin-AY-ah)—Don Quixote's name for Aldonza.

Samson Carrasco (SAM-son kah-RAS-ko)—Don Quixote's neighbor, who calls himself the Knight of the Mirrors and the Knight of the White Moon.

SETTING

Important Places

La Mancha (la MAHN-cha)—The province in Spain where Don Quixote lives.

El Toboso (el toe-BOH-soh)—The city where Dulcinea lives.

Barataria (bah-rah-TARE-ee-ah)—The island ruled by Sancho Panza.

Time Period

Don Quixote takes place during the late 16th century (the 1500s). During this time, Spain was a great world power. Its explorers had traveled all over "the New World" of the Americas and had claimed Mexico, Central America, most of the West Indies, western South America, and large sections of what is now the United States. Spain also controlled lands in Africa and Europe.

Many people in Spain were farmers at this time. Others lived in cities and worked as craftsmen or bought and sold the many products that came from Spain's far-flung empire.

The late 1500s were also a time of great creativity. Some of Spain's most famous and important books were written during this period, including *Don Quixote*. That is why this period is often called the Golden Age of Spanish Literature.

1
A Man with a Dream

Stand back, good friends, as I prepare to slay an evil dragon with my sword! 'Tis I, Wishbone, a brave knight, battling this round, shiny monster filled with...rotten food and trash? What's this upon the beast's head? A lid? This monster looks strangely like...a garbage can. You know what? It is a garbage can. Okay, so maybe I got carried away for a second. But if you think I have a wild imagination, you haven't met Don Quixote. Get set! We're going back to late 16th century Spain for the adventures of a man with an extraordinary imagination.

Alonso Quixana paced up and down in his room, pushing a bony hand through his graying hair. Quixana owned a farm, but he spent more time reading than he did working in his fields. Right now, his love of books was causing a big problem.

Quixana stopped pacing and turned to his niece and housekeeper.

"How can I get more books?" he asked. "I *must* have more books about knighthood!"

"Uncle," his niece said, trying to hold on to her

temper, "you've already filled the house with books. Just look at this room—your silly books are stacked to the ceiling!"

"Silly, you say?" Quixana roared. "Not my books, Niece. Each book is a wonderful adventure featuring some of the greatest men the world has ever known." Quixana waved his arms passionately. "These books tell of the tremendous strength and courage of knights. These men risked their lives in battle, fought evil to honor their beloved maidens, feared nothing and traveled everywhere! If these books are silly, then I am twice as silly."

"If the boot fits, wear it," the housekeeper whispered to herself.

"I need more!" Quixana said again. "But how can I pay for them?" Suddenly he laughed aloud in triumph. "I have the answer! I will sell some of my land and use the money to buy more books!"

"But Uncle—"

"My decision is made," Quixana said firmly. "Nothing is as important as my books. Soon I will be reading new stories filled with mystery, love, adventure, and the heroic deeds of my beloved knights."

Quixana did not waste any time. By the end of the week, he had sold the land and was reading again. In fact, he read day and night, barely eating or sleeping.

"I worry about my uncle," Quixana's niece told the housekeeper. "He is going to drive himself crazy with all these books about knights."

"If he doesn't drive *us* crazy first," the housekeeper pointed out.

To make matters worse, Quixana was not a quiet reader. He cheered loudly as the knights battled horrible monsters and evil magicians. He shouted warnings to his heroes when they faced a trap. He laughed triumphantly when a knight returned safely home from battle.

"That is the life to lead," Quixana said as he slammed a book shut, "and I am the one to lead it!"

Quixana looked around his small house and smiled. He walked over to his great-grandfather's old suit of armor which had hung on the wall for as long as anyone could remember. Quixana ran his hand over the rusty, bumpy metal. "Well, why not?" he said aloud. "With a little oil, this armor will be as good as new."

Then he went out to his barn and looked over his horse, Rozinante. His tail swished lazily back and forth, and his bones were clearly visible through his sparse brown hair. Quixana said, "He will do fine in battle."

Quixana hurried back to the house. "Niece!" he shouted as soon as he walked through the door.

His niece and the housekeeper ran to him.

"What is the matter, Uncle?" his niece asked anxiously.

"I have decided to become a knight," Quixana announced proudly.

"You're going to become a *what*?" asked his surprised niece.

"I must be losing my hearing," the housekeeper said in amazement. "Did you say you were going to become a knight?"

"I have no time to waste," Quixana continued. "I must oil that old suit of armor and put the finest saddle on Rozinante. I know there is a sword somewhere out in the barn. I will sharpen it until it glitters like gold. Stand aside, Niece—I am off to do battle with the foulest villains and scariest monsters in Spain!"

"The scariest thing in Spain is your brain," the housekeeper said boldly. **That's one funny housekeeper.**

But Quixana did not hear her. He was already dreaming of the adventures he was about to have.

"There are so many wrongs in the world that I can make right. I can battle giants who crush innocent farmers and rescue fellow knights who have been captured by enchanters. **Don Quixote believed enchanters could cast a spell over a knight and enchant or bewitch him. I can only be enchanted by one thing— large pepperoni pizzas with anchovies.** I will fill my life with danger and adventure, all in the name of doing good. I will dedicate my life as a knight to a fair maiden. All my victories will be for her."

Quixana thought of a young woman he knew from town, a girl named Aldonza. Stories of her long hair and dark eyes had charmed Quixana. Aldonza was only a simple peasant girl, but in Quixana's mind she was a beautiful maiden, a princess. There was just one problem—Aldonza didn't even know Quixana existed.

Quixana imagined the fair lady standing now in front of him, and he dropped down to one knee.

"Aldonza, from now on I will call you Dulcinea of El Toboso. I will tell everyone I meet that you are the fairest lady in all of Spain. Let no man ever say a bad word about you, or they will answer to me."

Next, Quixana said, "Now that I have a lady to dedicate my life to, I need a new name. 'Quixana' is not a proper name for a knight! I shall be called . . ."

It took Quixana eight days to think of a suitable name. Then he smiled and said, "I shall be known as Don Quixote." **"Don" is Spanish for "sir." A don is someone who has earned respect from others. Hmm... Don Wishbono. Not bad.** Then he remembered that knights usually added the name of their province to their name. Don Quixote stood tall and proud and declared, "From this day forth, I will be called Don Quixote of La Mancha, the bravest knight in the land."

So Alonso Quixana is now Don Quixote, and he's all set to be a knight. He's got his armor and his horse. Reading about knights is exciting, but being one is a totally different kind of adventure. It can be a lot tougher than it seems in books. Will Don Quixote's dreams of being a knight come true?

2
A Knight is Born

T he very next day, Don Quixote saddled Rozinante and set out on his journey, sure that he would soon find fame and fortune.

It was a boiling hot day in La Mancha. Don Quixote soon became quite warm encased in his suit of armor.

Even though the sweat poured down his face, Don Quixote's mind was fixed on a bigger problem. He was beginning to think that he had jumped into this knighthood business a little too quickly. "How can I call myself a knight when I have never been given that honor?" he asked himself as Rozinante paced wearily down the road. "In all the tales I've read, a knight must be dubbed by another knight in a special ceremony. I don't want to just say that I'm a knight—I want it to be official! After all, it wouldn't do to have just anyone call himself a knight! The answer is clear: I must find another knight!"

Find another knight? Sounds simple, but there's one minor problem: There haven't been knights roaming the land in Spain for at least a hundred years. Let's watch Don Quixote handle this.

Don Quixote rode all day down the dusty road, but there were no knights to be seen. By nightfall, both he and Rozinante were hungry and thirsty and covered with dirt from the road. At last, they came upon an inn.

"Aha!" Don Quixote cried. "Here is the castle of a great nobleman." Indeed, Don Quixote saw a grand fortress with high stone walls decorated with flags, not the tumbledown inn that it really was.

The innkeeper bustled out to greet him. "Good evening, great lord," Don Quixote said. "I desire to partake of your hospitality this evening."

"You mean you want dinner and a room?" the innkeeper asked in some confusion. "No problem."

"Please see that my steed is well cared for," Don Quixote requested. "He is a fine and noble beast, a fitting mount for my knightly journey."

The innkeeper cast a doubtful eye on Rozinante. The bony nag looked ready to collapse in a heap.

The innkeeper began to have his doubts about letting Don Quixote spend the night at his inn, but he wasn't about to turn away a customer. He led his guest inside and set a bowl of stew before him.

"Thank you, sir, for this magnificent feast," Don Quixote said when he finished the simple meal.

"Uh, right. So, Sir Knight," the innkeeper asked, "where are you going?"

To the innkeeper's astonishment, Don Quixote fell to his knees before him. "My lord, my name is Don Quixote of La Mancha, and I am performing good deeds to honor my lady, the beautiful Dulcinea of El Toboso. I have come here to ask you a favor. Please, it is my heart's deepest wish to become a knight! Only you can help me."

Everyone else in the room burst into laughter. But the innkeeper was a kind-hearted fellow. "Wait here," he said, motioning the others in the room to be quiet.

The innkeeper went to the kitchen and returned with a large carving knife. The guests pressed closer, not wanting to miss this ridiculous event.

"This is my sword," the innkeeper said, flashing the knife. "It has brought me great glory—"

"Yes, carving up roasts for dinner!" someone in the crowd shouted.

"—and I will be proud to knight you with it," the innkeeper continued, giving the loudmouth a dirty look. "Don Quixote, do you swear to uphold the knight's code of honor?"

"I do," Don Quixote promised. His voice held so much emotion, and his look was so earnest that the laughter in the room faded away.

"Then I dub you a knight," the innkeeper said. He touched the knife to Don Quixote's shoulders, first one and then the other. Everyone in the room burst into cheers.

"I thank you, good sir, for dubbing me a knight," Don Quixote said, rising awkwardly to his feet. "Now I can begin my adventures." He turned to go.

"Hey, wait a minute," the innkeeper said, suddenly remembering he was running a business here. "You have to pay for your dinner."

"Pay?" Don Quixote replied, honestly puzzled. "Good sir, a knight never bothers himself with money. We have much more important things on our minds."

"Knights may not think about money, but their squires do. You must have a squire to attend you and carry things such as money, food, and clothes."

"You are right," Don Quixote said, nodding at the innkeeper's wisdom. "And I think I know just the man."

The innkeeper decided that the experience of knighting Don Quixote had been worth a simple meal, so he sent Don Quixote on his way with many good wishes. **Knights get free meals? Maybe I should look into this...**

The next day Don Quixote rode to his neighbor's house. Now that he was officially a knight, he felt quite grand.

"Come out, good neighbor, and meet the knight who offers you a great opportunity," he shouted.

The door opened slowly. "I think you've got the wrong house," a voice mumbled from inside.

"No, no, Sancho Panza. It is *you* that I seek," Don Quixote assured him.

Sancho Panza peeked out from behind the door. He was a poor man who worked the fields for local farmers. He was as short and fat as Don Quixote was tall and thin, and he had dark, straggly hair and a big, droopy mustache. He knew nothing about knights and their adventures. But he knew plenty about Alonso Quixana.

"Quixana, you're crazy," Sancho stated. "Go

home and read your books and leave me alone."

"No, Señor Panza, I have stopped reading. Now I am doing! I am no longer Alonso Quixana. I am Don Quixote of La Mancha, the bravest knight in all of Spain! I will perform heroic deeds, and other men will write about *me*. But I need your help," Don Quixote added, sticking one foot in the door before Sancho could slam it shut.

"Sorry, I don't know how to write," Sancho said.

Back in Don Quixote's day, very few working people like Sancho went to school or learned how to read or write.

"I don't want you to write about me," Don Quixote said patiently. "I want you to ride with me. You will be my squire and assist me before I do battle."

"I don't have a horse, so I guess I won't be riding anywhere," Sancho said. "You can forget about doing battle. Do I look like a fighter to you?"

"You don't need a horse," Don Quixote said, "and you can leave the fighting to me."

Sancho still wasn't convinced. "Give me one good reason why I should go with you," he said.

"For the glory it will bring to your name," Don Quixote told him.

"My name will be Sancho Panza Glory? No, thanks. I like plain old Sancho Panza just fine."

"For the good of Spain, then," Don Quixote said.

"No offense, but Spain hasn't done much for me lately," Sancho argued.

"Then do it for the lands you will win," Don Quixote offered. "If you help me, one day I will give you an island, and you can rule it any way you like."

"An island? With me in charge?" Sancho liked the sound of that. Maybe if he had his own island, he wouldn't have to work so hard, and his wife would let him sleep late in the morning.

"Okay, Don Quixote," Sancho said finally. "I may be crazy too, but you've got yourself a *square*."

"Squire," Don Quixote corrected him.

"Oh, right, right. I mean squire," Sancho agreed.

The two men shook hands to seal their agreement.

"So, what should I do first?" Sancho asked.

"Be ready to travel by tomorrow morning. Prepare plenty of food and water for our journey. I will pay you for the supplies." Don Quixote took his squire by the shoulders. "Oh, Sancho, we will have great adventures, you and I, riding across Spain, bravely fighting any evil that comes our way."

"Remember, *you're* doing the fighting, not me," Sancho called out to Don Quixote as he rode away.

Don Quixote smiled as he set off merrily for home. Now he was truly a knight, complete with a squire. His adventures were about to begin.

I never knew it was so easy to get into the adventure business. Will knighthood be everything Don Quixote expects? We'll soon find out!

3

The Enchanted Windmills

Don Quixote learned about knights and their battles from books. But the creator of Don Quixote learned about fighting from experience. Miguel de Cervantes was a soldier long before he became a writer. In the 16th century, Cervantes fought in many battles. He was even captured once and spent five years as a slave. Eventually Cervantes put down his sword, picked up a pen, and created DON QUIXOTE. Hundreds of years later, the whole world still knows about Cervantes and his famous "knight."

The next day Sancho Panza rode his donkey, Dapple, to Don Quixote's house. Like his owner, Dapple was short and fat. He even had dark hairs around his muzzle that looked like Sancho's droopy mustache. The donkey plodded along the road, stopping every now and then to catch his breath.

Don Quixote watched as Sancho and Dapple waddled to a stop before him.

"What's the matter, Master?" Sancho asked.

"Your donkey, Squire—"

"Isn't he a beauty?"

"Well, yes," Don Quixote said, "but I have never read of a squire who rides a donkey. I do not know if it's allowed. I must do and say things exactly like the knights in my books."

Sancho's face sagged. "You mean I have to *walk*?"

Don Quixote thought for a moment. "No, I don't want to tire you before we even leave La Mancha. You can ride your donkey. When I defeat a knight in battle, you can take his horse."

Sancho brightened again. "Sounds good to me, Master. Are we ready to go?"

"Yes, devoted squire. The time has come. Great things await us!"

"Just as long as an island awaits me," Sancho said. "You haven't forgotten, have you?"

"A knight never breaks a promise. You shall have your island," Don Quixote assured him grandly.

The two set off down the road. Don Quixote rode

Rozinante, who was not quite the fine horse he thought he was. He'd spent many years grazing lazily in Don Quixote's fields and certainly wasn't used to carrying an armored knight. He looked as if he might collapse under Don Quixote at any moment. Sancho waddled along behind on Dapple.

The knight and his squire rode easily for some hours. Suddenly, Don Quixote stopped and sat up straight in his saddle, amazed at the sight before him. Thirty or forty massive giants stood in a field, glaring at the approaching knight. They hummed some evil song that made Don Quixote shiver. But despite his fear, he knew it was his duty to defeat them in battle.

"Look, Sancho, up ahead," Don Quixote said, bursting with excitement.

"What?" Sancho asked nervously. He wasn't ready for adventure quite so soon.

"See the giants with arms thirty feet long! There are so many that they almost cover the sky," Don Quixote whispered in awe. "And listen! Hear their song? They must be preparing for battle."

"Giants? All I see is a field full of windmills."

"No, Sancho," Don Quixote told him solemnly. "Can't you see all those wicked giants with long, white arms? They are clearly waiting to attack any innocent riders who may pass by. I must engage these giants in battle and save Spain from their evil ways."

Sancho stared at his master in disbelief. "Sir, I tell you, those are windmills! The long, white arms you see are sails that catch the wind. Their "song" is simply the creaking of the mills and the rushing of the wind."

Is Don Quixote right? Are these windmills really giants? Or are these giants really windmills?

But Don Quixote was not convinced. "You have much to learn, Squire," he said. Without waiting for a reply, he set his lance and charged straight at the nearest windmill.

A lance is a weapon knights used when they were on horseback. It's long and thin with a sharp steel tip.

"Do not try to escape me, you devilish giants. I have come to do battle!" he yelled.

Don Quixote's lance stabbed one of the sails. The lance pierced the cloth and stuck into it. The sail pulled both the knight and his horse to the ground, breaking the lance.

Rozinante quickly clambered to his feet. But Don Quixote lay motionless on the ground.

Sancho ran over to his master. "Are you all right? I told you they were windmills. You must have wind in your head," he chattered as he helped his master to his feet.

"Please, good Sancho, be still. There is a great trick at work here," Don Quixote said, genuinely puzzled.

"I wish I knew a great trick to keep you from getting killed," Sancho said.

Don Quixote slapped his forehead. "I know," he said. "Some evil magician turned those giants into windmills just as I attacked. He wanted to deny me a victory. The forces of evil are always after brave knights."

"If that's what you believe, then it must be true," Sancho said patiently although he was still sure of what *he* saw. "Here, let me help you back on your horse."

Don Quixote winced. His side ached. His knees wobbled so much he had to grab Sancho for support.

"You've got some nasty bruises from your fall," Sancho said.

"They are nothing," Don Quixote replied, breathing hard. "A knight receives many bruises in his quest for glory. But I've never read of a knight who complains about his injuries, so I must not complain."

"Does this rule about not complaining apply to squires too?" Sancho asked.

The knight scratched his head, trying to remember. "I have never read of that."

"Good. Then I'll feel free to yell and moan any time I get hurt," Sancho said with satisfaction.

Don Quixote laughed. Sancho's good nature helped the knight endure his pain. The two men rode a short distance and then spent the night under some trees, so Don Quixote could rest his bruised bones.

Don Quixote is a little bruised and battered on the outside, but inside he feels pretty good. He knows he gave it his best shot when he attacked those "giants." Don Quixote's desire to be a brave knight and his dreams of glory will lead to more problems.

4
A Battle on the Road

Like Don Quixote, many 16th-century Spaniards read books about knights and their code of chivalry. The code of chivalry required a knight to help the weak and battle the wicked. Cervantes knew about these books, and he thought they were, well, a little silly at times. He also thought people took them too seriously. Cervantes decided to write a parody of books about knighthood. A parody is a work that pokes fun at something by imitating it. In DON QUIXOTE, Cervantes pokes fun at the romantic adventures of knights. He also pokes fun at the people who get carried away reading them. "Carried away" certainly describes Don Quixote. Let's see how he handles the code of chivalry.

The next day Don Quixote and Sancho Panza set off again. The sun shone brightly, and the air was warm and pleasant.

"Something wonderful will happen to us today, good squire," said Don Quixote. "I can feel it."

Sancho looked up to the sky. "Please, Lord, don't

let us see any more windmills," he implored. He looked around nervously.

"No, there are no trick windmills before us today. But look, there is something else to stir a knight's blood." Don Quixote pointed toward a cloud of dust ahead of them. "Sancho, do you see?"

Sancho stopped riding and peered up the road. "I see two monks on donkeys in front of a carriage pulled by horses," he said. He didn't think there was anything very exciting about that.

"Sancho, your eyes deceive you," Don Quixote told him. He waved his sword in a sweeping arc before him. Sancho ducked as the blade whipped past his head. "Those men you think are monks are actually wizards. See their black robes? Villains always wore black in the old tales. In that carriage is a beautiful princess. These wicked magicians have kidnapped a fair maiden. It is my duty, under the code of chivalry, to rescue her."

With a flourish, Don Quixote took out his broken lance. That morning he had snapped a withered branch off an oak tree and tied it to the lance to replace its damaged tip. Don Quixote was not worried. In his eyes, his lance was as strong and sharp as before. **Don Quixote had read about this little trick in one of his books. Unfortunately, Don Quixote's branch was more of a twig.**

"This is going to be worse than the windmills," Sancho said to himself.

The monks were only a short distance away. They

rode in silence, the hoods of their robes pulled tightly around their heads. They did not see the knight and his squire waiting for them on the road.

"Foul-minded magicians, I give you one chance to release the princess you have captured," Don Quixote called to the monks. "But if you deny my request, you will feel the point of my lance in your belly."

The two monks stopped short when they spotted Don Quixote holding his lance. The monks exchanged quizzical looks. It was clear they had no idea what Don Quixote was talking about.

"Sir Knight," said the first monk nervously, "we are just two simple monks returning to our monastery. We know nothing about magicians and captured princesses."

"Very well," Don Quixote said fiercely, "you have sealed your fate."

Sancho Panza knew there was trouble ahead. "They are monks," he told Don Quixote. "Monks, not magicians!"

Don Quixote did not seem to hear him. "I cannot wait a moment longer," he cried. "Release your prisoner, or feel my blade!"

Don Quixote spurred Rozinante forward. The monks looked in horror as Don Quixote charged at them. Don Quixote's ridiculous-looking lance missed the first monk, but the man fell off his donkey in fear. He crawled to the side of the road and scuttled away, terrified.

The second monk didn't wait for Don Quixote to

charge him. He and his donkey ran off faster than the wind, kicking up a cloud of dust.

"Run, wicked men, and bother these good people no more!" Don Quixote yelled after them.

Don Quixote approached the carriage. There were two men and two women inside. They gazed at Don Quixote in fear and surprise. But Don Quixote had eyes only for a beautiful young lady with large, dark brown eyes and wavy brown hair that fell across her shoulders.

"Ah, fair princess," Don Quixote said with a bow, "I have saved you from the evil magicians who captured you. You and your party are free. You do not have to thank me. All I ask is that you go to El Toboso. There, it would please me if you would find the most beautiful Dulcinea, the light of my life. **Remember Dulcinea? That's Don Quixote's fancy name for Aldonza, the peasant girl he's in love with.** Tell her how I, Don Quixote of La Mancha, have saved you. Let her know that all the good deeds I do are for her." Don Quixote bowed again as he finished his speech.

A man in the coach burst out laughing. He was quite the gentleman in his fine suit and equally fine leather hat. When the man stopped laughing, he looked down his pointy nose at Don Quixote.

"You are a madman," the man exclaimed. "She's no princess. You didn't save anybody from anything, and we're certainly not going to El Toboso. I have important business in Biscayne, and *that* is where we are going."

"Good sir, I was speaking to the lady," Don Quixote said quietly but firmly.

The man got down from the coach and faced Don Quixote. He was as tall as Don Quixote but had much broader and stronger shoulders with arms like tree trunks.

"I am not your good sir, you fool," he bellowed.

"If you were a gentleman," Don Quixote said, "perhaps I would reply to you. But you are not."

"Me? Not a gentleman?" The man drew his sword. "No one dares to insult me so."

"I believe my master just did," Sancho said helpfully. He quickly

Ooh, I don't think it's a good idea for him to make Don Quixote angry.

moved back as Don Quixote drew his sword too.

"Sir, you are about to fight a most brave and fierce knight," Don Quixote announced.

"Oh, really?" the man said haughtily. "You mean you have another knight hiding in the woods who will take your place?"

Don Quixote's face turned red as his anger boiled. "I'll give you one last chance to put away your—"

Before Don Quixote could finish, the man swung his sword. It whirred through the air and clanged against Don Quixote's armor. Only the steel plating he wore kept Don Quixote from losing his arm.

"Oh, Dulcinea!" Don Quixote cried. "Pray for your faithful knight who is in great danger!"

The men's swords hissed through the air, clanking against each other in resounding blows. They glittered brightly in the sun, flashing and dancing. Sancho Panza could only stare in wonder at this spectacle. At last, Don Quixote saw his chance. He brought his sword down with all his might. With a tremendous *thwack*, the flat side of his blade smacked the man's head and knocked him to the ground.

The man moaned as he grabbed his head. When he pulled his hands away, blood stained his fingers. His moans grew louder.

Don Quixote leaped to the ground and held the tip of his sword against the man's throat. The man whimpered like a lost dog, his eyes wide with terror.

"Spare him! Please!" a sweet voice called.

Don Quixote turned. The beautiful young woman leaned out of the carriage. The breeze caught her hair, making it shimmer in the sun. Her eyes spilled tears.

"Kind knight, please spare him," she begged.

Don Quixote pulled back his sword and bowed to the woman.

"I cannot refuse a lady's request," Don Quixote said. "I will grant your wish and spare this man's life. But I have a request to make in return—that you go to El Toboso, as I asked. There, you will find my beloved Dulcinea, the fairest princess in all of Spain. Tell her of me and what you have seen today. I fight every day in her name." He bowed again as he finished his speech.

The woman hastily agreed to Don Quixote's request. Meanwhile, Don Quixote's beaten opponent rose and hurried back into the carriage. The driver immediately turned the carriage around and raced down the road.

"You didn't kill him," Sancho said in wonder.

"Because of chivalry, Squire. A knight cannot refuse the request of a royal lady."

Sancho Panza was proud of his master. He had fought bravely. Don Quixote had been right—that man wasn't a gentleman, no matter how much money he had. He was a bully.

"My arm is sore from the blows I took," Don Quixote said. "I think I will need to rest before we travel much further."

"Maybe there's an inn nearby. Come on, Master,

let's get going," Sancho said, trying to sound lighthearted.

Sancho Panza and Don Quixote laughed and talked as they rode. Again and again, they described what had happened, relishing every detail of their victory.

Their long day of adventure was finally over.

Or so they thought.

Don Quixote isn't the only one who confronts the forces of evil. I have to deal with cats and dog catchers almost every day. Now, what new adventure is in store for our brave knight? Will it be something wonderful—or something terrible?

Helllooo! Start flipping the book pages and check out the action.... Woo-cha!

5

A Rough Night
at the Inn

What exactly is a novel? It's a story someone creates using his or her imagination. Another meaning of the word novel is something that is new or different. When Miguel de Cervantes wrote DON QUIXOTE, he wrote a "novel" novel. Historians call DON QUIXOTE the first novel written in Europe. People had created long tales with one or two main characters, but these were poems or stories passed on by word of mouth, not read. So while you're reading, remember: you're holding a piece of history in your paws.

After riding for a few hours, Sancho Panza and an exhausted Don Quixote came upon a shabby building with a stable next to it.

"We're in luck," Sancho said. "This looks like an inn where we can spend the night."

"Yes, this looks like a fine castle. I'm sure its lord will gladly welcome a gallant knight and his squire," Don Quixote said confidently.

"Castle? Did I say 'castle'?" Sancho looked around.

"This is an inn. It's not too big, and it's a little shabby, but it's definitely an inn—you know, a place where travelers can eat and sleep."

"Sancho, this is a castle," Don Quixote said sternly. "I'm sure it would not please our host to hear you insult his home by calling it shabby. Ah, here comes the fellow now."

An older man with gray hair approached as Sancho helped Don Quixote down from his horse.

"Do you gentlemen need a bed for the night?" he asked, rubbing his hands together expectantly.

"Yes, good sir. I am weary from battle and would like to rest," Don Quixote replied.

"I'm not feeling so great myself," Sancho admitted.

"You'll have to sleep in a room with some other guests," the innkeeper said.

"My lord, whatever space you have will suit us just fine," Don Quixote answered humbly. "We need to spend just one night in your castle. We'll be on our way in the morning."

The innkeeper raised his eyebrows and looked at Sancho. "Did he say 'castle'?"

Sancho shrugged. "My master believes your simple inn is a great castle," he said.

"Okay, whatever you say," the innkeeper agreed. "Maritornes! Come show these men to their room."

A young girl came out of the inn. She was barefoot and wore a simple peasant dress. She took one of

Sancho's saddlebags and led the two adventurers inside.

"What happened to him?" Maritornes asked Sancho, looking at Don Quixote with concern.

"He was wounded in battle," Sancho told her.

"Battle? Is he a soldier?" the girl wondered.

"He is no common soldier," Sancho replied proudly. "My master is Don Quixote of La Mancha, a chivalrous knight."

Maritornes looked puzzled. "Night? It's not yet sundown."

Sancho shook his head. "You poor, simple girl, I don't mean after sundown. I mean a *knight*. My master travels the country looking for adventure and confronting evil. Someday he will be a great king." Sancho leaned closer to the girl and confided, "He's promised me my own island, you know."

"That's nice," the girl said, frowning. She decided not to ask any more questions of this odd pair.

Don Quixote looked around him and smiled. "I must compliment you on your fine castle," he said. "I have never seen such high, thick walls, and the stonework around the gate is masterfully done. Even the king must envy you."

"Huh?" Now the girl was totally confused.

Sancho winked at her. "He just finished a tough fight. Took a blow to the head. He's not himself."

"Oh," the girl said, still looking strangely at Don Quixote. "Well, here's your room. Grab any bed you can find."

"You call these beds?" Sancho cried. Rows of thin pieces of wood covered with worn straw and ripped burlap bags filled the room.

"These will suit us just fine, Sancho," Don Quixote said. "My body is sore and tired. Though I would prefer downy feathers or silken sheets, these beds will do."

Sancho and Don Quixote picked out two empty beds and lay down. The room was quiet at first. But as darkness fell, the room filled with travelers.

"Ow!" Sancho cried as someone stepped on his hand.

"Sorry," a voice muttered.

Another traveler stumbled into Don Quixote's bed.

"Good sir, please step with caution," Don Quixote said as politely as possible.

"Hey!" Sancho shouted as someone almost sat on his head. "Go find your own bed. This one's taken." He buried his head under the flimsy pillow.

The comings and goings of the other guests went on for hours. Things had no sooner quieted down when Maritornes, the servant girl, came into the room carrying water. She stumbled in the darkness and practically fell into Don Quixote's arms.

"Oh, excuse me," she said, flustered.

"Ah, good lady. I regret that your affection cannot be returned. My heart is dedicated to sweet Dulcinea," Don Quixote said as he helped the girl to her feet.

"What are you talking about?" Maritornes asked.

"I know it is hard to face the fact that I cannot

love you back, but I must live by my oath to Dulcinea."

Maritornes was outraged as she realized what Don Quixote was talking about. "Look, mister, I was just coming up here to bring some water," she snapped.

"Hey, Maritornes, is that you?" A large, broad-shouldered man strolled over to join her by Don Quixote's bed. His beefy arms strained against the sleeves of his shirt.

"Yeah. This guy in armor is bothering me," Maritornes told him.

"Oh, yeah?" The man gave Don Quixote a whack on the head. Don Quixote tumbled back onto his bed.

"You are a brute, sir," Don Quixote said weakly. "Be thankful my sword is not near my side, or else..." The brave knight's voice trailed into silence.

"What kind of inn is this?" Sancho demanded angrily. "Can't a squire get some sleep?"

"I think this castle is enchanted," Don Quixote said. "I'm having the strangest dreams. I dreamed the lady of the castle came to me, begging for my affection. Of course, I told her all about my devotion to Dulcinea. A minute later, I imagined a giant came into the room and struck me on the head while I slept."

"I'm glad someone in here slept," Sancho said bitterly.

"Well, now I will rest again. It is a funny place, this castle," Don Quixote mused.

• • • • •

Sancho was up at sunrise. He yawned, still tired after his restless night. Don Quixote, however, was clearly ready to find new adventures.

Don Quixote and his squire prepared to set out on their journey. The innkeeper approached just as the knight was swinging himself onto Rozinante's back.

"Good sir," Don Quixote said, "I must thank you for your hospitality. I slept and ate well."

"I'm glad to hear that," the innkeeper said. "Now all you have to do is pay your bill."

Don Quixote didn't remember reading about knights paying bills after staying in castles. "My lord, it is common for the owner of a castle to let a knight and his squire stay free of charge," he explained.

"That's great for people who own castles, but I'm running an inn here. People pay to stay under my roof," the innkeeper said firmly.

"I'm afraid I have no money to pay you. Knights like me are too busy thinking about fighting monsters and rescuing maidens to worry about money. Good day to you." Don Quixote rode off.

Meanwhile, Sancho was struggling to get on Dapple.

"Not so fast, Mr. Squire," the innkeeper said, laying a hand on Sancho's arm. "One of you must pay."

"You know that rule about not paying?" Sancho said hurriedly. "I'm sure it applies to faithful squires too, so I'll just be—"

Suddenly, the huge man who had hit Don Quixote the night before stepped forward to block Sancho's way. His big, burly friends were right behind him, and they didn't look too friendly.

"Is this guy causing trouble?" the man asked the innkeeper, thumping Sancho on the chest.

"Yeah. He and his friend won't pay their bill," the innkeeper shouted.

"So you're trying to cheat an honest innkeeper, eh?" The man reached out and yanked Sancho right off his donkey. Dapple decided he didn't want any part of this and trotted down the road.

"Come on, boys, lend me a hand," the man said with a nasty laugh. The muscles in his arms rippled as he held Sancho high in the air.

"Uh, sir," Sancho whispered politely, "your hand is a little tight around my throat. I really prefer to have my feet on the ground, if you don't mind. I don't like heights."

"Did you hear that?" the man shouted to his friends. "He doesn't like heights. Isn't that a shame."

The other men laughed. "Maybe we should show him some real heights," one of the men cried.

Someone grabbed a blanket off a nearby horse. Each man grasped a corner of the blanket. The huge man heaved Sancho into the middle of the blanket, and the men began tossing him into the air.

"This is really lots of fun," Sancho said, "but I...oh...AYYYEEEE!"

Sancho bounced higher and higher. The tops of the trees whirled past his dizzy eyes. A blackbird on a branch squawked at Sancho, wondering what he was doing so high in the air. Every time he fell, Sancho feared he'd smash into the ground. But the blanket always caught him—and then sent him soaring toward the sky again.

"Maybe we'll shake some money out of him," one man joked.

Sure enough, coins began falling out of Sancho's pockets.

"Come on, stop," Sancho begged. "That's all the money I have, honest. Please, stop!"

The men laughed. They kept right on tossing Sancho until their arms grew tired. Then at a sign from the big brute, everyone dropped the blanket. Sancho fell to the ground with a thud. The innkeeper and the men returned to the inn, still laughing.

Sancho stumbled to his feet, his head still spinning. His eyes focused on Don Quixote trotting down the road. "Master! Wait for me!" Sancho called as he hurried to grab Dapple's reins.

I once spent a day at the pound, but that inn was brutal! Now what about poor Sancho? Being tossed into the air is a rough way to start the day. But I guess that's the life of a squire: doing all the dirty work for knights. I just hope he can catch up with Don Quixote.

6
At War with the Sheep

Sancho Panza is one tired puppy. His little bounce on the blanket left him exhausted, sore, and a little angry at his master for leaving without him. But as Sancho soon learns, the code of chivalry has some strange rules.

S ancho struggled onto Dapple and rode toward Don Quixote, who was waiting for him some distance down the road.

"Sancho, I told you that castle was enchanted. What happened to you is proof," Don Quixote said with awe. "Ghosts caused you to fly into the air!"

"No, they were real people, all right," Sancho assured him. "I've got the bruises to prove it."

"The magic affected me as well. I wanted to ride back and help you, but something kept me and Rozinante from moving," Don Quixote continued. "We were stuck as if in ice."

"Oh, sure, it was magic. *That's* why you didn't help," Sancho said sarcastically.

"Even without such magic, I could not have helped you," Don Quixote said solemnly.

"Why's that?" Sancho was almost afraid to ask, but his curiosity got the better of him.

"The code of chivalry," Don Quixote replied as if that explained everything.

"I thought the code told you to help people in trouble," Sancho said irritably.

"You are right," Don Quixote said. "But the code also says a knight can only fight another knight or a person of high ranking."

"Well, I'm sure ghosts aren't as noble as knights or wizards," Sancho said, rolling his eyes. "They certainly aren't up to your high standards."

"I fear not," Don Quixote said.

Sancho looked Don Quixote straight in the eye. "Master, I've been thinking, maybe it's time for us to go home. We're not getting much out of these adventures except a lot of bumps and bruises."

"How little you know of knighthood, Sancho!" Don Quixote was clearly shocked at the very idea of going home. "This is a noble calling, and it will pay its rewards. Someday, you will have your island, and I will win glory for the fair Dulcinea."

Sancho shook his head. "I still think we should go home, work the fields, and mind our own business."

"Sancho, sometimes a man has to think big. My books of knighthood filled me with a great dream—to ride across Spain and battle evil wherever it may be. To become a knight, I left my family, gave up my comfortable life, and entered an unknown world of adventure and danger. But all my sacrifices are nothing because I am doing what I believe I was always meant to do. You are helping me fulfill my dream. For that, I am most grateful."

"I'm also getting beaten up while I help," Sancho reminded his master, wincing.

"It's true. Sometimes a knight's life—or a squire's—is hard. But things will get better for us. I am sure of it."

As Don Quixote and Sancho rode along, a huge cloud of dust rolled in front of them.

"Sancho, do you see what I see?"

"Probably not," Sancho muttered.

Don Quixote didn't hear him. "Here is my chance to show once again the might of my sword and my bravery in battle. This swirl of dust is from an army marching this way. When an army is marching, a battle is close at hand."

"There must be two armies around here," Sancho said. "There's another cloud of dust over there." He pointed the other way.

Don Quixote turned and saw the cloud approaching from the opposite direction.

"Two armies are about to do battle," he said with great excitement. "They will meet right in front of us in that field. Sancho, this is a great day!"

"What are you going to do?" Sancho asked worriedly.

"I will choose the side that most needs my help and fight with skill and courage. It is what a good knight must do," Don Quixote told him.

The two men waited for the armies to draw near. Through the dust, Sancho noticed something strange about the armies. The soldiers had four legs. They were small and covered in white, woolly fluff. Was this another illusion by some nearby enchanter?

"Don Quixote, before you rush into battle—"

"Yes, Squire?" Don Quixote gave Sancho a stern look.

"I have to tell you, those soldiers are sheep!"

"Do not make fun of them, Sancho. All soldiers must follow orders and move as if in a herd," Don Quixote said, frowning at Sancho's lack of respect.

"No, I mean they're *real* sheep," Sancho insisted. "Covered in wool. Baaaa! You know—sheep!"

"Ah, Sancho, you are so easily deceived," Don Quixote said with great pity. "Look, over there I see Laurcalio, a great lord of Spain. There, in yellow armor, is the knight known as Micocolembo." Don Quixote went on naming the great knights he imagined he saw in front of them.

"Listen," Don Quixote urged Sancho, "don't you hear the clang of armor, the sound of marching feet, the beat of drums?"

"All I hear is sheep," Sancho said stubbornly.

"Sancho, I understand your fear of this impending battle. This fear is clouding your senses, making you see and hear things that are not there. My senses are as sharp as my sword—and now it is time to use it!"

"But—" Before Sancho could finish, Don Quixote pointed Rozinante toward the nearest dust cloud.

"Ho, good knights!" Don Quixote shouted. "I come to help you fight the forces of evil."

Sancho watched as Don Quixote rode into the flock of sheep. The knight swung his sword this way and that, scattering sheep in all directions.

Then Sancho heard a noise. It sounded like big raindrops hitting a metal roof. Puzzled, he looked up the hill and saw the shepherds who tended the two flocks of sheep running toward them.

"Master! Look out! The shepherds have slingshots!" Sancho called.

Don Quixote ignored his squire's cry. "Come, Sir Knight, do not run," he called to the flock of sheep. "Fight me bravely as the code of chivalry requires!"

From the hill, the shepherds unleashed round after round of stones, but they bounced harmlessly off Don Quixote's armor.

"See, Sancho, I have nothing to fear," Don Quixote yelled. "These little blows cannot—"

THUNK!

A rock hit Don Quixote squarely on the forehead. He wobbled in his saddle, and tumbled to the ground. Yelling and cursing, the shepherds ran down the hill, rounded up their sheep, and hurried away.

Sancho approached his fallen master, who was sprawled out on the ground with his eyes closed. "Are you all right?" he asked.

"I did not see the knight who hit me, but surely he is an evil man and a dirty fighter," Don Quixote said.

"Are you hurt?" Sancho asked, worried.

"I think not," Don Quixote said slowly, reaching for his helmet. "But look, my helmet is cracked."

"I'm afraid the helmet's not the only thing that might be cracked," Sancho couldn't help saying.

"A knight cannot fight without a helmet," Don Quixote said sadly. "We cannot go on until I replace it."

"Where are we going to get a helmet out here?" Sancho demanded.

"I don't know, Sancho, but I have faith," was Don Quixote's simple reply. "We will find one. Until then, we will eat and rest."

Sancho saw a dark cloud in the sky. It was moving fast—and headed in their direction.

"I don't think this is the best place to rest," Sancho warned.

"Why not?" Don Quixote inquired.

At that moment, the heavens opened, and it began to pour rain onto their weary bones.

"That's why."

Okay, let's review. So far, the brave Don Quixote has been knocked flat by a windmill, scared a couple of unsuspecting monks, been knocked around in his sleep by a bully, and he's just finished a battle with sheep. What could possibly top that? Well, turn the page to find out.

7

Mambrino's Helmet

As if Don Quixote and Sancho don't have enough problems, now it's raining. But even bad weather can't dampen Don Quixote's spirits—or stop him from replacing his broken helmet. In fact, Don Quixote knows exactly what he wants in a new helmet as we're about to see.

Don Quixote and Sancho Panza sat dismally in the rain, huddled under a blanket. The dampness made Sancho's bruised bones ache, and the rain made puddles by his feet. Don Quixote turned to him, shaking his head.

"You see, Sancho, this is one reason why a knight must always have a helmet. With a helmet, I could ride without my head getting wet. This is so undignified."

"Here's an idea—you could find shelter and wait for the rain to stop," Sancho pointed out.

"I know I will find a helmet soon," Don Quixote said with great certainty. "It will not be just any helmet. It will be Mambrino's helmet."

"Sombrero's helmet?" Sancho asked.

"*Mambrino,*" Don Quixote repeated. "He was an evil king who lived long ago. A brave Spanish knight, Rinaldo, battled the king and took the helmet as a prize. Mambrino's helmet is made of gold, and it is said to have magical powers. It has been passed on from knight to knight. I believe it is now my turn to have this helmet."

"A magical helmet made of gold?" Sancho asked with a scowl. "I've never heard of anything like that."

"That's because you have never read about knights and their chivalrous deeds."

"So we have to sit out here in the rain while you wait for a magic helmet to show up?" Sancho couldn't believe it. Things were going from bad to worse.

"We will find it, Sancho, never fear." Don Quixote looked down the road. "See, Sancho, we don't have to wait long. Look at what is approaching."

"All I see is a man on a donkey, and he's wearing something on his head," Sancho said wearily.

"Again you are wrong, Squire," Don Quixote declared. "That is no ordinary man. It is an evil knight on his warhorse, and that something on his head is Mambrino's helmet! See, even under the dark skies, the gold shines brightly. It is just as grand as the writers described in my books! The helmet is mine by right, and I will have it."

Don Quixote took out his lance and climbed on Rozinante. "Stop, knight, and tell me who you are before I do battle with you," he shouted.

The rider, a bearded man dressed in plain clothes, looked startled. "Me? I am just a simple barber. I ride from town to town making my living cutting hair and healing the sick. **In Don Quixote's day, barbers didn't just cut hair. They also performed surgery and treated wounds.** It's not much of a living, I can tell you. Why do you want to battle *me*?"

"So, you deny that you are a knight," Don Quixote barked. "Then, what is that on your head, if not the famous helmet of Mambrino?"

"This?" The man knocked on the so-called helmet and laughed. "This is my wash basin. I fill it with water when it's time to shave my customers. When it started raining, I put it on my head."

"You might fool others with these lies, but you will not fool Don Quixote. Defend yourself, thief, or else hand me the helmet only a good knight deserves to wear."

Don Quixote gripped his lance tightly and aimed it right at the barber's chest. Then he urged Rozinante into a gallop and charged. The barber was so scared he fell off his donkey. Before Don Quixote could reach him, the barber ran away as fast as his legs would take him. The wash basin fell off his head and bounced along the road.

"Another victory!" Don Quixote cried. "The helmet of gold is mine."

Sancho picked up the basin and knocked it with his fist. "You mean the pot of lead. This is a wash basin, just as the barber said."

"It is Mambrino's helmet, the finest helmet in all of Spain. Give it to me!" Don Quixote commanded.

Don Quixote took the pot and put it on his head, but it slid down over his face. Sancho began to laugh uncontrollably.

"Why are you laughing?" Don Quixote said with great dignity.

"I'm sorry, Master," Sancho said between giggles, "but the 'helmet' is just a little big for you."

Don Quixote pushed up the pot so he could see. "When we reach a village, I will ask the blacksmith to make it fit better. But now that I have my helmet, we can go on."

See how strong Don Quixote's imagination is? Where others see a lead pot, Don Quixote sees the golden helmet of Mambrino. Sancho thinks it's lead, but then Sancho hasn't read all those books about knighthood.

Meanwhile, Sancho was looking through the barber's things.

"You know, this man had a nice saddlebag," Sancho said, "and I left mine behind at the...uh...enchanted castle."

"Are you saying we should take the bag?" Don Quixote asked, eyebrows raised in surprise.

"Could I? I mean, if it's okay with the code," Sancho added hastily.

Don Quixote thought a moment. "I know that a knight who wins a battle is allowed to take the loser's possessions. But can a squire remove something as well? I am not sure. Until I learn otherwise, I say yes, you may take the bag."

Sancho was as happy with his new bag as Don Quixote was with his new helmet. Together they continued down the road.

8
Don Quixote Loses His Mind

Don Quixote is happy with his helmet, and Sancho is pleased for his master. But as the two ride for days without finding any new adventures, Don Quixote gets upset. He worries he's not doing enough to honor his beloved Dulcinea of El Toboso. Thinking about her and his dreams of glory, he decides he wants to ride in silence. So he commands Sancho not to speak unless Don Quixote speaks to him first. Imagine a talkative squire like Sancho trying to keep quiet! Let's see how long that lasts.

Don Quixote and Sancho Panza rode into some nearby mountains. Dapple and Rozinante slowly picked their way over rocky trails and narrow cliffs. Don Quixote murmured quietly to himself about his beloved Dulcinea. Sancho, however, rode silently, obeying his master's command not to speak.

After a few hours, Sancho began to squirm. He closed his eyes tightly and bit his lip. Not talking was more than he could bear! He knew that sometimes he spoke out of turn and annoyed his master, but this was too much. Sancho prayed that Don Quixote would speak to him about something, *anything,* just so he could reply.

Finally, Sancho couldn't take it any longer. "Master, you must allow me to return home," he blurted. "At least with my wife and children, I can talk all day long, and no one ever minds. If you want me to travel by your side and never open my mouth again, you might as well bury me alive because this is worse than death. It would be one thing if Dapple could talk—at least I could whisper to him as we rode along. But he's no magical beast. It's bad enough seeking adventures and getting tossed in the air and beaten and bruised along the way, but not talking is killing me!"

Sancho took a deep breath after his outburst. He waited for his master to yell at him or send him home. Instead, Don Quixote stopped riding. He slowly turned to face his squire, and he smiled.

"I understand, Sancho," Don Quixote said slowly. "I forgot how hard it is to travel so long without speaking. Friends need to talk to each other. I will allow you to speak—"

"Oh, thank you, Master!" Sancho cried gratefully.

"—for now," Don Quixote continued. "As long as we are in the mountains, you may speak whenever you like."

"What happens when we get through them?" Sancho asked hesitantly.

"I will decide then whether to ban you from speaking again or let you converse freely. It all depends on my next plan."

"Uh-oh," Sancho muttered under his breath.

"Did you say something?" Don Quixote asked sharply.

"Nothing, Master. I can't wait to hear your plan. You know how I love your plans. So what is it, Don Quixote?"

"I have been thinking that my fair Dulcinea may not have heard of all the brave things I am doing in her name," Don Quixote said. "I have no guarantee that the people I sent to her actually went to El Toboso." Don Quixote rested his chin in his hand. "I recall a story about a knight who went mad," he continued. **Is the knight who "went mad" angry at someone? No, in this case the word "mad" means that the knight has lost his reason, or his sense of logic, and is acting a little strange. We'll see how strange Don Quixote acts when he pretends to be "mad."** "He was so far from his lady, and he did not know if her love for him still burned bright. So I see that I have no choice. From now on, I will be mad—until I hear from my lady, Dulcinea."

Now Sancho was really confused. "Master, excuse me for asking, but is there a good reason for pretending to be mad?"

"It is what knights do when they are wandering far from their true loves. It is in all the books I have read," Don Quixote declared.

"Well, it certainly sounds mad to me," Sancho said with a sigh. "So, Master, what can I do to help you?"

"You, good squire, are going to take a letter to Dulcinea," Don Quixote answered.

Don Quixote went through his pack and pulled out a book.

"I will write the letter on a blank page in this," Don Quixote told him. "When you come to a town, find someone who can copy it in the very best handwriting onto the most elegant writing paper. Then, take the finished letter to the loveliest woman in all of Spain: the shy daughter of Lorenzo Corcuelo—my fair Dulcinea."

Sancho jumped. "The daughter of Lorenzo Corcuelo? *That's* who Dulcinea of El Toboso is? I've always known her as Aldonza Lorenzo."

"They are one and the same," Don Quixote said, sweeping his hand before him dramatically. "I prefer to call her Dulcinea, and I know she is really a lady of royal blood."

"Oh, yeah, that Aldonza is a riot," Sancho said, smiling as he remembered the girl. "She can arm wrestle like a farm hand, and she loves to sing songs around the fire, and can she tell a joke! She's one of the funniest young women in the village."

"Yes, she has many fine qualities," Don Quixote said severely. "A lady as fair as my Dulcinea would never arm wrestle. She is as dainty and beautiful as any woman who has ever walked the earth."

"Of course, Don Quixote," Sancho said, nodding. "Anything you say, Master."

Don Quixote sat down and began writing the letter. When he was finished, he looked up and spotted

Sancho stretched out under a nearby tree, his hat tilted low over his eyes.

"Sancho," Don Quixote called. "Come here and let me read this to you. I want you to memorize it in case you lose the book along the way."

"You trust my memory?" Sancho asked as he hurried over. "I sure don't. But read it anyway. I'm sure it's very beautiful."

Clearing his throat, Don Quixote began to read:

Most beautiful and beloved lady,
I lay wounded and mad from love, so far from you and your grace. I send you wishes of good health and happiness, though I myself cannot enjoy these things

without you. My good squire, Sancho, will describe my
sadness in great detail. Please, tell him what you would do
with me. If you can ever love me, I will be yours forever. If
you cast me aside, I will have no more purpose for living and
will be forced to bury my love with my body.

    Yours until death,
    Don Quixote of La Mancha

Sancho wiped a tear from his
eye. "That's the most wonderful
thing I've ever heard," he sobbed. "I
wish I could write something like
that."

"It is all part of being a
knight, Sancho," Don
Quixote said serenely.
"One must have a
strong body *and* a tender
heart. Now, take the letter
and make haste for El Toboso.
You may ride Rozinante to speed you on
your journey."

"What will you do while I am gone, Master?"

"I will practice being mad. I will act like the knight
in the story and tear off my clothes, scatter them about,
throw my armor into the trees, and bang my head
against the rocks. My madness will amaze you!"

"Oh, maybe, maybe not," Sancho said, biting back
a grin.

"Perhaps, you should see what I plan to do," Don

Quixote said. "Then you can tell Dulcinea exactly what my condition is."

"No, really, that's okay," Sancho said hastily. "I can use my imagination."

"No, Sancho, I think you should," Don Quixote insisted.

"All right, if you insist. But be careful with those rocks. I don't want to come back and see that you've banged your head a little too hard."

"Don't worry, Sancho, I will be very much alive when you return," Don Quixote promised.

Sancho climbed aboard Rozinante and watched Don Quixote take off his armor, and then his shirt and undershirt. As he shouted nonsense and waved his arms, he ran among the trees half-naked, doing somersaults and leaping from one foot to the other. Sancho shook his head.

"I think," Sancho said, patting Rozinante, "our master has got this madness bit down pretty well."

Fighting evil and turning somersaults? Sancho is constantly amazed at how demanding the knight business is. So what will happen next? Will Sancho find Dulcinea—I mean, Aldonza—I mean, what's-her-name? Will she profess her love for Don Quixote? How can Don Quixote be a knight in not-so-shining armor if he's running around with no clothes? Keep reading to find out!

9

A Little Help from My Friends

While Don Quixote stays in the wilderness, Sancho rides down the mountain and heads for El Toboso. The next day, he comes upon a building that seems very familiar —too familiar. In fact, just looking at it makes Sancho tremble with fear.

Sancho pulled Rozinante to a halt and watched people going in and out of the building by the roadside. He could see many horses tied to the posts outside. The building seemed a little run-down: chipped pieces of stone lay around the walls, and there were a few holes in the roof.

"This place looks awfully familiar," Sancho said to himself. "Did my master and I pass this way?"

Sancho rode closer. Suddenly he realized the building was an inn—and not just any inn. It was *the* inn.

"Oh, no!" Sancho cried. "This is that terrible place where those goons tossed me to the sky in a blanket! I'm not going in there, not for a million pieces of gold."

But Sancho's stomach rumbled and grumbled. *It* didn't remember the blanket episode—it just wanted food. Sancho hadn't eaten a warm meal in days. He remembered the fine food he had eaten at the inn and licked his hungry lips.

Just then, Sancho saw two travelers leave the inn. They looked very familiar. The two men seemed to recognize Sancho as well.

"Friend Sancho Panza!" said the first man, a fellow with neatly trimmed, graying hair. He carried a small pack on his shoulder. "Imagine running into you out here!"

Sancho realized this was the barber from La Mancha.

"Where is your master, Quixana?" asked the second man whom Sancho recognized as the village curate. He wore a long black robe and a white collar, and a pair of tiny glasses sat on his nose.

A curate is a priest or minister, someone in charge of a church.

Sancho was glad to see two friendly faces, especially at this unfriendly inn. But he was reluctant to tell them what he was doing now.

"My master, umm, my master is..." Sancho searched for the words. "He's...on a secret mission! Yes, a secret mission for a local duke. It's very hush-hush. I can't tell you any more."

The two men burst out laughing.

"Come on, Sancho," the barber said. "We know Quixana, or should I say 'Don Quixote of La Mancha.'

Isn't that what he's calling himself now? You'll have to tell us a better lie than that."

"Yes," said the curate, "or else we'll think you've done something terrible to him, like beaten him and stolen his horse."

"You know I'm no thief," Sancho said indignantly. His feelings were hurt. "All right, I'll tell you the truth. I left him in the mountains, running around like a madman. He is suffering for love of Dulcinea of El Toboso."

"Now that sounds more like the Don Quixote we know," the barber said, nodding.

"Why is he doing that?" the curate asked.

Sancho shrugged. "He read about it in one of his books on chivalry. It's what knights do when they long for their maidens, I guess. I don't ask too many questions anymore."

"So what are you doing here while your master is in the mountains?" asked the barber.

"I'm on a mission. Don Quixote wants me to deliver a letter to his love. I'm supposed to find somebody with neat handwriting to copy it over. Hey, Father, you're an educated man," Sancho said to the curate. "Maybe you can do it for me. I've got it right here—" Sancho put his hand into his pocket, then took it out. "—right here..." He began wildly patting his pockets. "I know I...where the...oh, no! This can't be true!"

Sancho started frantically throwing things out of

his pack. He looked under his saddle and even in his boots.

"I lost it! I lost the letter. My master is going to kill me. It was such a beautiful letter too."

"Did you read it?" the curate asked.

"No, but my master read it to me. He wanted me to memorize it in case I lost the letter. That's it! I'll see if I can remember it, and then you can write it down for me. Will you do that, Father?"

"Of course, Sancho," the curate replied. He went to his horse and took paper and pen out of his pack.

"Let's see..." Sancho closed his eyes and tried to remember. "I think it started 'Bedeviled lady.'"

"I think perhaps you mean 'Beloved lady'?" the curate suggested.

"Yeah, yeah, that's it. 'Beloved lady, blah, blah, blah. I hope you're well. I'm not. I'm sick and crazy without you. The world's greatest squire, Sancho Panza, will tell you what's what. Tell him what you think of me. If you love me, great. If you don't, I will throw myself off the rocks and splatter all over. Without you, I have no porpoise.'"

"'Purpose'?" the curate interrupted.

"Right. 'Purpose. Signed, Don Quixote of La Mancha.'"

"That's it?"

"That pretty much says it all, don't you think? Hey, thanks a lot, Father. I really appreciate your help."

"My pleasure, Sancho." The curate looked at the

barber. Then he asked the question both men were wondering about. "Tell me, Sancho, why do you follow Don Quixote? Do you believe all his talk of knights and their adventures?"

Sancho thought a moment. "I believe that he really believes it, and by believing, he does some good deeds—or tries to anyway. I know we've had *real* adventures, exciting ones. My master *is* a good man, and he treats me well. I don't always understand his dreams of glory or his imagination, but I'm starting to think having a dream, imagining what might be, is a pretty good thing. Besides, he's promised me my own island to rule. Don Quixote could become an emperor someday or at least a king. Stranger things have happened."

Sancho has the scars to prove it.

The barber leaned over and whispered to the curate. "The only strange thing here is our neighbor. He's starting to sound like his master. These dreams of Don Quixote are powerful things."

The curate nodded and then smiled as he turned back to Sancho. "Your loyalty is a fine thing. But your master will never win any lands or titles while he's running around in the wild. You should convince him to leave the mountains and find food and shelter."

"That's right," the barber agreed. "You don't want Don Quixote to run off a cliff or smack into a tree. You'd better do something."

Sancho *was* worried about his master's health. "What can I do? He won't budge until he hears from Dulcinea."

"You could take a letter back from Dulcinea today," the barber suggested slyly.

"Today! That's impossible. How can I get to El Toboso and back today?"

"You won't even have to leave the inn. We can write it for you. I'll make up the words, and Father will write them down."

Sancho put his hands on his hips. He was shocked at their suggestion. "You want me to deceive my master?" He looked at the curate. "Do you agree to this, Father?"

"You're not trying to hurt your master, Sancho," the curate said. "Your master's health is very important, isn't it?"

"Yes, of course," Sancho readily agreed.

"Then I think you should do as our friend suggests."

"All right," Sancho finally said although he still had his doubts. "If you say it's okay."

The two men quickly wrote a letter begging Don Quixote to leave the mountains and come to El Toboso. They signed it "Your devoted lady, Dulcinea." Then they handed the letter to Sancho.

"I'm still not sure about this," Sancho said doubtfully.

"Trust us, Sancho," the curate assured him. "Your master could be in great danger otherwise."

"You don't want anything bad to happen to Don Quixote, do you?" the barber asked.

"Oh, no," Sancho insisted.

"Then this is what you must do," the barber said.

Sancho smiled uncertainly. "I guess you're right," he said, sounding a bit more confident as he thought the matter over. "This should do the trick. My master will be off that mountain in no time. Thanks for all your help." The squire got on Rozinante and prepared to head back to Don Quixote.

"Is there any message you'd like us to bring back to La Mancha?" the curate asked.

Sancho thought for a moment. "Tell my wife I miss her cooking," he finally said.

"Your wife is a good cook?" asked the barber.

Sancho made a face. "She's terrible. But right now, I'm so hungry even one of her meals would seem like a feast. See you around."

I bet you thought Sancho was going to run into trouble at the inn. I know I did. Instead, he met some old friends who gave him a hand. Now, can Sancho really convince Don Quixote that he met the fair lady? We'll soon find out.

10
Sancho Plays a Trick

Sancho Panza heads back up the mountain with a note from Dulcinea. Will Don Quixote believe Sancho has been to El Toboso and met the fair lady of his dreams?

Sancho Panza rode as fast as he could to the place where he had left Don Quixote. He rode most of the night and arrived early the next morning. Sancho found Dapple tied to a tree, and he saw some of Don Quixote's belongings scattered about. However, his master was nowhere in sight.

"Where'd he go running off to?" Sancho muttered to himself. Sancho searched behind rocks and under fallen trees for his missing master.

"Don Quixote!" Sancho called frantically. "Master, where are you? It's Sancho. I'm back from El Toboso, and I have good news!"

"Sancho? Is it really you?" A weak voice called.

"Master! Where are you?"

"Here, Sancho, here!"

Sancho followed the voice to a nearby stream. There, lying by the water, his face in the mud, was Don Quixote. The knight wore only a tattered shirt, and he looked worn and thin.

"Master, what are you doing?" Sancho asked with concern.

"Look in the water," Don Quixote replied. "I can see the face of my fair Dulcinea."

Sancho pulled Don Quixote away from the stream and propped him against a tree. "Master, it's time to end your madness," he told him. "I have good news from Dulcinea."

"Dulcinea, my adored lady," Don Quixote sighed. "I am not worthy of her love."

"Sure you are," Sancho said, smiling. "She thinks you're the greatest knight ever to slide into a suit of armor. It's all in this letter she sent you."

Don Quixote's head began to clear. "You saw her? She wrote a letter?"

"That's what I've been trying to tell you," Sancho said impatiently. "Here, read it."

"I cannot read in this state," Don Quixote said wearily. "My head is dizzy from hunger, and my madness has exhausted me. You must read it to me, Sancho."

"You know I can't read."

"Then tell me everything," Don Quixote said. "Tell me everything that happened in El Toboso, every word my fair maiden said. What did you say to her? What did she say when she read my letter? Who copied the letter for you?"

"Slow down, slow down!" Sancho shouted. "First, I have to tell you something because I always tell you the truth." Sancho crossed his fingers behind his back. "Nobody copied the letter. I lost it."

"I know," Don Quixote replied. "I found it on the ground after you left. I was very upset to see it. Why didn't you return for it?"

"I didn't need to," Sancho said. "I had learned the letter by heart; it was so beautiful. I met a curate on the road, and I repeated the letter to him. He wrote it down, and then I brought it to Dulcinea."

"Go on," Don Quixote demanded. "Tell me more. What was she doing when you arrived? Was she stringing pearls for a necklace or knitting a dainty sweater?"

"Actually, she was..." Sancho paused, trying to think of what to say. "She was working in the fields cutting down wheat. Yes, that's right!"

"A lady who is not afraid of honest labor. I like that. If only I could eat the bread made from the wheat cut by her hands!"

"Anyway, I tried to give her the letter," Sancho continued, "and she told me to put it down on the ground."

"Ah, she wanted to read it later when she was alone, so she could savor every word," Don Quixote said knowingly.

"Then," Sancho went on, "I told her about the condition you were in, how mad you were without her love. She was impressed with your devotion. But she told me—she also wrote this in the letter—that you should leave the mountain and ride to El Toboso."

"This is better than I could have expected!" Don Quixote shouted with glee. "But there is one thing I don't understand, Sancho. You left only a few days ago, yet you have been to El Toboso and returned. It is quite extraordinary."

Uh-oh. Has Don Quixote figured out what's going on? Is Sancho's well-intentioned trick going to be discovered?

Sancho thought fast. "Well, Master, you see..."

"It is fortunate that every good knight has a helpful magician who looks after him," Don Quixote said. "All the books on knighthood talk of such powerful wizards. The magician must have put a spell on you, so you and Rozinante could fly like the wind."

Sancho sighed with relief. "That's just what I was going to say, Master. I was indeed fortunate. I felt like some strange magical force was at work the whole time I was away."

Don Quixote leaped to his feet, now filled with energy. "What should I do about Dulcinea's request?"

"Do?" Sancho said with disbelief. "Are you kidding? Grab your clothes, get your armor, and let's go!"

"No, Sancho, I'm not sure that is the best thing to do," the knight said. "On one hand, I long to see my lady. But on the other hand, I wonder if I should do more good deeds in her name. I must be truly worthy of her affection before I can bow down before her."

Sancho was growing impatient. "Master, that's

nonsense. You're plenty worthy now. You're the worthiest knight I know. Think of all the brave and kindhearted things you've done in her name. She wants to see you, so you should go and see her!"

Don Quixote shook his head. "If only it were that simple. You still do not completely understand the laws of chivalry, Sancho. Many good knights have professed their love for a woman as beautiful and good as Dulcinea. Many have also won favor, yet they did not run to the lady's side at once. I must continue my quest to help those in need. **Do you know what "quest" means? A quest is a mission to find or do something special. Don Quixote's quest is to be a noble knight and to honor Dulcinea. That's a pretty tall order.** But I will travel in a direction that takes us toward El Toboso."

"So you'll get dressed and get back on Rozinante?" Sancho asked anxiously.

"Yes, good squire, my madness is over. I shall return to the life of a knight!"

Sancho looked up to the heavens and clasped his hands together. "Thank you, good Lord," he said fervently. "You have answered my prayers!"

So Don Quixote and Sancho pack up their things and ride down the mountain. Sancho's trick had worked! Don Quixote was safe, for now.

11
Don Quixote
Goes Home

A lot of people don't know it, but Miguel de Cervantes wrote two books about Don Quixote. The first one was published in 1605. After the success of DON QUIXOTE, Cervantes wrote Part Two. What you've read so far all happened in Part One. At this point in the story, a lot of time has gone by. Don Quixote and Sancho are making a quick stop back at La Mancha before they set out to continue Don Quixote's quest. Let's join our two heroes as we begin the second part of DON QUIXOTE.

D on Quixote lay in his bed as his niece brought him plates of food. It felt strange to lie on a soft mattress after sleeping so many nights on the hard earth.

"Uncle, I'm so glad you're home!" Don Quixote's niece said with a huge grin. "I worried about you the whole time you were away."

"Niece, you have nothing to fear while I am out seeking adventure," Don Quixote assured her. "With my sword and my lance, I defeat all manner of evil beasts and wizards."

Don Quixote's niece was so happy to see her

uncle, she could not stop smiling. "Let us feed you and bathe you, and then you can rest. Tomorrow we can go out to the fields and—"

Don Quixote was puzzled. "Do you think I returned to work in my fields? Oh, no, Niece, I just stopped in to say hello. I will take the time to eat this meal, but then my squire and I must return to our travels."

The smile disappeared from his niece's face. Now her lips trembled as she tried to hold back tears.

"Oh, Uncle! You can't mean you're going to leave us again. It's bad enough that you read so many books about knights. Now you have that squire filling your head with wild ideas."

"I never liked that Sancho Panza," the housekeeper agreed. "He has beady eyes."

Just then, someone knocked at the door. When the housekeeper opened it, Sancho Panza walked in.

"You!" the housekeeper shouted. "You think you're going to take Señor Quixana away from his home again? Get out of here, Sancho Panza."

The niece joined the housekeeper. Together they tried to close the door on Sancho.

"Hey, is that...oof...any way...to treat...ouch...your uncle's friend?" Sancho demanded as he pushed against the door.

"Some friend," the niece said. "You encourage my uncle to seek these crazy adventures. You're a bad influence!"

"Niece!" Don Quixote shouted. "This is still my house. Invite Sancho Panza in."

The two women stepped back from the door. Sancho, who was still pushing against it, tumbled to the floor. He sat there dazed, rubbing his head.

"We haven't even left yet, and I've already got bruises," the squire complained.

"Uncle, are you really leaving again?" his niece asked.

Don Quixote nodded. "My quest for glory is not yet complete. I have more to do as I play my small part in bringing chivalry to the world." Don Quixote hugged his niece. She burst into tears and clutched her uncle. Pushing her away gently, Don Quixote grabbed his sword and headed outside to saddle Rozinante. Sancho stood up, brushed himself off, and then bowed deeply to the two women. The housekeeper gave him a dirty look.

"Take good care of my uncle!" Don Quixote's niece cried.

"I always do, good lady. We take care of each other."

Don Quixote was already sitting on Rozinante. He waited impatiently for Sancho to mount Dapple.

"Are you ready for more adventure, good squire?"

"You know, I really am," Sancho said, a little surprised at himself. "The whole time we were home, I thought about your dream and how important it is to you. I guess it's becoming important to me too."

Don Quixote nodded, proud of his squire. Then he asked, "Tell me, Sancho, when you walked through the village, did you hear people talking of me?"

"Yes, Master," Sancho replied.

Don Quixote leaned forward eagerly in his saddle. "What did they say?"

"Well, Master," Sancho said slowly, "some think you're doing a great thing by trying to live a chivalrous life."

"They are correct," Don Quixote said, beaming.

"Unfortunately, most say you're just a crazy old fool, and I'm no better," Sancho admitted. "But who cares what people say, right?"

"You are very wise to think so, Squire. Many great people have been called mad for what they did or what they believed. But when a person has a goal, he cannot let anyone's words stop him. Nothing will stop us."

Great. Don Quixote prepares for more adventures, while I'm chained in a dungeon, prisoner of an evil witch! Oh, foul deed! These chains are... Wait a minute. Helllooo. This dungeon smells almost exactly like my yard. Funny thing too—this chain looks a lot like my leash. Well, nobody can tie Don Quixote down. Now he's more determined than ever to make his dreams of chivalry a reality. He knows he has a good friend by his side—a friend who will stand by him, no matter what happens. What awaits our brave knight and his squire? We'll soon find out!

12

A Plot against Don Quixote

Shortly after Don Quixote set off on his latest adventure, his niece, his housekeeper, and some friends got together. They were worried about Don Quixote.

"What are we going to do?" Don Quixote's niece asked. "My uncle still insists he is a knight, and he's been off traveling around Spain for months. Now he's left again. I'm so worried about him."

"That no-good peasant Sancho Panza is with him too," the housekeeper added. "Who knows what trouble he'll get my master into?"

"I wouldn't worry too much about Sancho," the curate said, "From what he told us, Quixana is as crazy as can be."

"I have an idea. We can give him potions and medicine," offered another neighbor. "Maybe they will clear his mind and convince him he is truly Alonso Quixana and not this knight, Don Quixote."

"No," the curate said. "I have a better plan. Our friend truly thinks he is a knight. So only another knight will be able to convince him to stop his travels."

"Oh, that's a great idea," said the housekeeper. "We'll just pick any old knight who's lying around to do this. We have *so* many knights in our village."

"I know there are no knights here. But I also know someone who will help us. One of our neighbors, Samson Carrasco, has agreed to dress as a knight. He will ride after Don Quixote, insult him, and then do battle. When Samson beats Don Quixote, he will be forced to return to La Mancha and put away his armor. Don Quixote will have to obey. The code of chivalry dictates it." The curate smiled at his own clever plan.

"I don't know," the niece said. "It sounds risky. What if my uncle wins?"

The others all laughed uproariously at the very idea. "We don't have to worry about that," the priest assured her. "Samson is young and strong. Your uncle is...well...you know your uncle."

Don Quixote's niece was not entirely happy with this plan, but at last she reluctantly agreed: They would send Samson Carrasco after Don Quixote.

Now let's return to Don Quixote and Sancho. They've been riding all day long, and now they're resting by the side of the road.

Sancho Panza leaned against a tree, ready for a long nap. Don Quixote also closed his eyes, but the sound of hoofbeats brought him wide awake. He looked down the road and saw a man in armor—another knight! This knight had a squire too. The two men dismounted and tied their animals to a tree.

"Wake up, Sancho!" Don Quixote nudged his squire, greatly excited. "We are about to have an adventure." Don Quixote pointed down the road.

"All I see is a guy in armor and a short, fat guy with a donkey. There must be plenty of guys like that around. Where's the adventure?" Sancho asked wearily.

"It may not be a great adventure, but I think it could be the start of one," Don Quixote insisted.

"Well, why don't—"

"Shh! Silence, Sancho. The knight is about to speak to his squire. Let us see if we can hear what he has to say," Don Quixote whispered.

Back in the 16th and 17th centuries, writers often used rhymes to tell a story. Sometimes the rhymes were poems, and sometimes they were songs.

> *"I search the earth and heaven above*
> *For something as beautiful as my love.*
> *And though I know not where thou art,*
> *My feelings are real, deep in my heart.*
> *I'm a brave knight, strong and true,*
> *And all my battles I fight for you.*
> *To you no other lady does compare—*
> *Let no one say another is as fair."*

When he finished, the knight sighed loudly and sat under a tree.

"Ooh, this knight has got it bad," Sancho said. "Sounds like he's in love."

"All knights are in love," Don Quixote replied sharply. His face was red with anger. "This man is in error. Unless he sings about my Dulcinea, he dares not say another is more beautiful than she. He cannot be singing about my Dulcinea, for only I have her love."

"Maybe you should go over and talk to him," Sancho advised.

"Good idea, Sancho. Let us go."

As he approached the knight, Don Quixote could see he was a young man, tall and strong. Sancho carefully looked over the knight's squire, starting from his feet and working up to his...nose. Sancho zeroed in on the nose.

"Master, check out the nose on that squire. Poor guy. It's hideous! So red and long."

"Quiet, Sancho. He might hear you and take offense. Let me speak for the two of us.

"Good day, good knight," Don Quixote addressed the man. "I see we are brothers in the life of chivalry."

"Yes. I am glad to meet a fellow knight. I am the Knight of the Mirrors. I am called this because in battle my armor shines like so many polished mirrors."

"My squire and I heard your song. It was filled

with lovely words, but your words are false. No woman can match the beauty of my own lady."

The Knight of the Mirrors laughed defiantly. "I sing only the truth. My lady, Casildea of Vandalia, has no match for beauty in all of Spain. It is for her that I have beaten all the knights I meet. I have even beaten the famous Don Quixote of La Mancha."

Sancho's mouth dropped open. "Did you hear, Master? How can he say such a—"

"Quiet, Squire. I will deal with this." Don Quixote's voice was steely.

The Knight of the Mirrors laughed again. "What kind of knight is this who lets his squire speak without first being spoken to? I have much more control over my squire, as you can see."

Sancho looked at the other squire. "You sap," Sancho sneered, "I wouldn't let you feed my donkey."

"Silence!" Don Quixote thundered. "Good sir, it is not right to say this to a fellow knight, but I must speak the truth: You lie. You have not beaten Don Quixote."

"Oh, but I have," the knight replied. "Is he not a skinny old man who rides a broken-down horse? And his squire, Sancho Panza, is he not a fat slob —"

"What?" Sancho cried.

"—with a brain no bigger than his donkey's?"

"Why, I oughta—" Sancho clenched his fists.

"This Don Quixote," the knight continued, "fights in the name of Dulcinea of El Toboso, whom he claims is the fairest maiden in all of Spain. But the world knows the fairest is my Casildea. Oh yes, I have beaten that Don Quixote."

"Are you going to let him get away with this?" Sancho asked his master, practically jumping up and down in outrage.

"No, Sancho, you are right. I cannot let this outrage go on." Don Quixote stood up tall and proud. "Sir, *I* am Don Quixote of La Mancha, and I will not let you say such things about Dulcinea or myself."

"I take this as a challenge to do battle," the Knight of the Mirrors said.

"It is indeed," Don Quixote said solemnly.

"Then I accept."

"Shall we fight tomorrow morning by the sun's first rays?" Don Quixote suggested.

"Agreed."

The Knight of the Mirrors turned and walked to his horse, smiling to himself. "I have him now," the knight thought. "I will win the battle and send Don Quixote home where he belongs!"

Send Don Quixote home? This must be Samson Carrasco, the neighbor sent by Don Quixote's niece and friends! Don Quixote's been pretty lucky so far, fighting barbers and shepherds. But how will he do against another knight? Okay, so it's just Carrasco pretending to be a knight. But he is young and strong. Will Carrasco beat Don Quixote and send him back to La Mancha?

13

A Stunning Victory

Don Quixote and Samson Carrasco—also known as the Knight of the Mirrors—are about to joust. A joust is a fight between two knights on horseback. They face each other at a distance and then charge at each other. They use their lances to try to knock each other off their horses. We've never seen Don Quixote joust with another knight before. Will his first time be his last?

As the sun rose the next morning, Sancho Panza carefully prepared Don Quixote for battle. Across the field where the joust was to take place, the big-nosed squire did the same for his master.

"He looks strong," Sancho said, his eyes on Don Quixote's opponent. "*Really* strong. That lance of his is pretty long and thick. I'd hate to get poked with that."

"It is not you who has to worry," Don Quixote said. "I am not afraid. I will defeat this knight and defend my honor—and the fair name of Dulcinea."

At last it was time for the joust to begin. Don Quixote and the Knight of the Mirrors approached each other.

"What are the terms of this battle?" Don Quixote asked.

"The loser shall do whatever the winner desires as long as it is allowed under the code of chivalry. Is this agreeable to you?"

"It is."

Don Quixote walked over to Rozinante and climbed into the saddle. The old horse whinnied nervously. He knew something important was about to happen.

Don Quixote's opponent mounted his horse as well. The two knights began to ride in opposite directions, so they would be the required distance apart at the beginning of the joust.

"Master," Sancho said as Don Quixote rode near him, "I want a good view of the joust. Will you help me get up this tree?"

Don Quixote sighed in exasperation. "All right. Come up here quickly."

Sancho climbed onto Rozinante, and Don Quixote helped boost his squire into the tree.

"Careful," Sancho said, straining to reach the next branch. "Just a little higher...."

At the other end of the field, the Knight of the Mirrors had already begun his charge. The knight steadied his lance as his horse's powerful legs galloped across the ground.

"Uh-oh," Sancho said. "I think the joust is starting without you."

Don Quixote was still holding onto Sancho's leg. "That cannot be," he cried. "I am not ready."

The Knight of the Mirrors finally saw that Don Quixote was still struggling with Sancho. He pulled hard on the reins of his horse, and the animal thundered to a stop just as Don Quixote finally shoved Sancho into the tree. Thinking his opponent was still charging him, Don Quixote rode toward the knight as fast as Rozinante could carry him.

"Come, Rozinante, run as you never have before," Don Quixote coaxed him. The old horse did exactly as he was asked. He raced at a speed neither Sancho nor Don Quixote had ever seen. Meanwhile, the Knight of the Mirrors tried to get his horse moving again, but the animal wouldn't budge.

"In the name of Dulcinea, prepare for my lance!" Don Quixote yelled as Rozinante thundered along at

top speed. An energy he had never felt before ran through Don Quixote's body. He aimed his lance at his opponent's chest. It hit the Knight of the Mirrors squarely and sent him flying off his horse.

"I don't believe it!" Sancho yelled, climbing down the tree as fast as he could. He ran over to stand beside Don Quixote at the fallen knight's side.

"Is he dead?" Sancho asked.

Don Quixote struggled to remove the knight's dented helmet. Then he and Sancho stared in disbelief at the young man's face.

"Hey, I know this guy!" Sancho exclaimed. "But it can't be."

"A magician has been at work again," Don Quixote said in wonder. "This knight looks just like my neighbor, Samson Carrasco."

"These magicians follow you everywhere. Maybe if you kill this enchanted being, you'll kill the magician too," Sancho suggested.

"What an excellent idea." Don Quixote drew his sword and prepared to run it through his beaten opponent.

"Wait!"

They turned and saw the other squire hurrying toward them. "He really is Carrasco," the squire explained. "And I am also your neighbor, Cecial." The squire yanked off his huge nose, which was actually a disguise.

At that moment, Carrasco came to his senses. Don Quixote, who had not been listening to a word Cecial had said, put his sword to Carrasco's throat.

"Confess, knight. Say that Dulcinea of El Toboso is the fairest of all, or I will end your life. And confess too that you did not win a victory over Don Quixote of La Mancha."

"All that you say is true," Carrasco agreed.

"Finally, admit that some enchanter changed your face so that you look like my neighbor, Samson Carrasco. This enchanter also changed your squire so that, without his huge nose, he looks like Cecial."

"Yes, yes. Anything you say," the young man said quickly, bobbing his head up and down.

Don Quixote put away his sword. "Good. You have met my terms of victory. Come, Sancho, let us continue our journey. Good day, Sir Knight."

Sancho proudly helped Don Quixote back onto Rozinante. This time, his master had not battled some giant or wizard conjured up by his imagination. He had defeated a real knight!

"You were so courageous, Master," Sancho said with awe. "He could have killed you. "

"I had to defend our honor, and the honor of Dulcinea," Don Quixote said nobly. "You should know by now that I am always striving to match the chivalry of the famous knights in my books. It was my duty to fight bravely."

"You always *talk* about chivalry and duty, but this

time you really did it by sparing his life," Sancho said, impressed.

"It's all part of the code, Sancho. I could do no less."

"Maybe there's more to this chivalry business then I thought," Sancho said to himself. But he was still a little puzzled. Was the Knight of the Mirrors really Carrasco? Or was a magician at work? In the end, Sancho dutifully decided to believe his master and not his own eyes. After all, Don Quixote knew a lot more about this knight business than he did.

Satisfied, Sancho got on Dapple and followed Don Quixote down the road.

Back in the field, the fallen Carrasco sat in the tall grass and held his bruised chest.

"I have lost this fight, Don Quixote, but the war is not over," Carrasco said with a burning anger. "Forget about my bargain with your niece. Now I am determined to beat you for my own sweet revenge!"

Ooh, Samson must have bruised his ego as well as some other things when he fell off that horse. Seems as if he's as wrapped up in being a knight as Don Quixote is. At least everything worked out okay for Don Quixote and Sancho—for now. But what will happen when Samson Carrasco tries to get his revenge?

14
Journey to El Toboso

Don Quixote and Sancho feel pretty good about things after Don Quixote's battle with the Knight of the Mirrors. With his latest victory, Don Quixote is now ready to take a break from his chivalrous duties and make a slight detour—to El Toboso.

For days, Don Quixote rode proudly in his saddle, describing over and over how he took his lance and knocked the Knight of the Mirrors right off his horse. Each time Sancho cheered as if he were watching the scene for the first time.

One day, Don Quixote brought Rozinante to a halt. "I've been thinking, Sancho," he said.

"Yes, Master?" Sancho said warily.

"I should grant the wish of my fair Dulcinea and visit her in El Toboso."

"El Toboso?" Sancho yelled. "I thought you had more battles to win and people to help before you could go to El Toboso. Maybe we should wait."

"Squire, you are strange. When I was muddled with craziness in the mountains, you said I should ride immediately to see Dulcinea. Now you want to delay. What is the matter?" Don Quixote inquired.

"Nothing, Master, nothing," Sancho said quickly. Under his breath, he muttered, "Nothing I can tell *you*." Sancho feared that if they rode to El Toboso, Don Quixote would learn about the lie Sancho had told him in the mountains.

"When we get there," Don Quixote continued, "you can lead me to Dulcinea's castle, since you know where she lives."

"Uh, sure, Master, I'll take you right there." Sancho shuddered as he imagined Don Quixote's anger when he learned he had been deceived. Of course, Sancho felt badly that he had deceived Don Quixote. But he thought it had been for his own good.

Don Quixote set off in the direction of El Toboso with a light heart. Sancho straggled along behind. After two uneventful days of riding, Don Quixote suddenly stopped in his tracks.

"Look up ahead!" Don Quixote said excitedly. "There are the gates of El Toboso."

Sancho gulped as he saw the city's massive gates and the church steeples rising above them.

"Oh, yeah, the gates of El Toboso," Sancho mumbled weakly. To himself he said, "I've got to stall. I've got to come up with a plan."

Back then cities had gates so the people could keep out invading armies and other bad guys.

"Uh, Don Quixote," Sancho said aloud. "Last time I was here, I was told it's the custom for visitors to enter El

Toboso after midnight. It's said the moon's glow makes the city especially beautiful."

Don Quixote looked puzzled. "That is certainly a strange custom. And it is a long time to wait to find Dulcinea. But I certainly am not one to disobey the customs of my hosts. We will wait, then, until midnight. Then you can lead me to Dulcinea."

Sancho slumped in his saddle. "Of course, Master. Anything you say."

Just after midnight, the two adventurers entered El Toboso. The city streets were quiet. The moonlight did indeed shine brightly on the streets—too brightly for Sancho's taste. If it were dark, he thought, he would have an excuse for not finding Dulcinea.

"You take the lead, Sancho," said Don Quixote. "Show me the way to the palace of my fair Dulcinea. Perhaps, she senses my presence nearby and lies awake, waiting for me."

"Actually," Sancho said hesitantly, "she wasn't living in a palace when I saw her."

"No? Then it was a small cottage where she lived alone with her maids."

"Nope. It was more like an, uh, alleyway."

"An alleyway?" Don Quixote exploded. "You are crazy, Squire. Who builds a castle or royal palace in an alley? What princess would live there?"

"Hey, I didn't build the place—I just found it," Sancho said defensively. "This city has lots of strange customs. Why can't they put their princesses in an alley if they want? Look, you're getting me upset. I'll never find the way to Dulcinea's if you keep this up!"

Don Quixote quickly bowed his head. "I apologize, Sancho. You are right; a guide does not need any distractions."

"Hey, I have a great idea," Sancho said. "You go back outside the gates and wait by those oak trees we passed a few miles back. After I find Dulcinea's palace, I'll come back and get you."

Don Quixote shook his head. "I don't know, Sancho. Now that I am so close to her, I don't want to delay seeing her for another minute."

"You've already waited for months, Master," Sancho said. "What's a little while longer? Besides, you must have seen her a thousand times in your knightly career."

"I have told you before, Squire, I have never seen the fair Dulcinea. It is only by her reputation that I know of Dulcinea's beauty and wit."

"So you've never seen her?" Sancho asked incredulously. He looked at the sky. "Just look at all the time we've wasted. The sun will be up soon. Come on. I'll go with you to the woods. Then I'll head back to look for Dulcinea."

"Agreed, Sancho." Don Quixote patted Sancho on the shoulder. "You are a good friend, and a most dedicated squire. You will have your reward some day."

"Yeah," Sancho muttered. "It will probably be a good, swift kick."

15
A Magical Meeting

Sancho really had to think fast to stay one step ahead of Don Quixote. But the squire's troubles aren't over. He has to find Dulcinea while Don Quixote waits outside of El Toboso. And he'll have to come up with a good story for Don Quixote if he doesn't.

At daybreak, Sancho prepared to leave Don Quixote.

"You know what you are to do?" Don Quixote asked.

"I know," Sancho said, nodding. "Tell her about your undying love, and beg her to let you glimpse her beauty."

"Yes, Sancho, that is it. Pay close attention to how she greets you. Note everything she says and does: Does she smile when you mention my name? Does she brush her face with her hand, or—"

"I get it, I get it!" Sancho shouted. "I'll be right back."

Sancho kept looking back as he rode, smiling and waving at his master. But as soon as he turned the corner and Don Quixote was finally out of sight, Sancho jumped off Dapple and fell to the ground. "Oh, why me?" he yelled, beating the earth with his fists.

Finally, Sancho calmed himself. He began a conversation with a voice inside his head.

"So, tell me, Sancho," the voice said, "where do you think you're going?"

"I'm going to El Toboso," Sancho replied.

"And why are you going there?"

"To find a princess for my master."

"Oh, no problem," the voice mocked him. "All you have to do is open up the first door you see and a princess will be waiting for you."

"Look," Sancho said angrily to the voice, "I never said this was going to be easy."

"You know Aldonza is not the princess Dulcinea."

"I know that," Sancho replied. "There is no Dulcinea, except in my master's wild imagination. I'll have to find another princess instead."

"If you do find a princess, do you think the people of El Toboso are going to let you cart her off to satisfy some old knight?" the voice went on.

"Hmm, I didn't think of that. What do you think they'd do to me?"

"Think about all the bruises and knocks to the head you've gotten so far—then multiply them by ten. You'll be lucky to drag yourself out of there alive."

Sancho winced. "I don't think I can deal with *that*. What am I going to do?"

Poor Sancho is so upset, he's talking to himself. Part of him knows he has an impossible task ahead of him. But the other part knows he can't disappoint Don Quixote by not finding Dulcinea. Finally, one part of Sancho finds an answer for the other.

"Okay, Sancho, you know Don Quixote is a little...crazy sometimes," the voice pointed out.

"Crazy? I used to think he was crazy, just like everybody else does. But now I like to think that my master just has a really vivid imagination."

The voice grew impatient. "Call it what you want. Anyway, if he's so quick to believe that something he sees is really something else, maybe that can help you."

Sancho liked the sound of that. But he wasn't sure exactly what the voice meant. "Keep talking," he told it.

"Say you find a peasant girl. You say to Don Quixote, 'Here is your beautiful Dulcinea.' He looks at her and says, 'Yes, it is she!'"

"But what if he says, 'This is just some peasant girl'?" Sancho asked.

"You say, 'Oh, no, Master, one of those terrible enchanters we keep running into has turned Dulcinea into a peasant girl.'"

Sancho thought for moment. "This could work," he said.

"It *will* work," the voice insisted. Then, its job done, the voice faded back into Sancho's brain.

Sancho sat by the roadside for a while so his

master would think he was searching El Toboso for the lady Dulcinea. Then, just as he was about to put his plan into action, Sancho saw three peasant girls riding donkeys toward him.

"How's that for luck?" Sancho said to himself. "I didn't even have to go looking for my Dulcinea, and I get three for the price of one."

He jumped on Dapple and rode back to his master. Don Quixote straightened in his saddle as he saw Sancho approach.

"Good news, Master! I have found her," Sancho said proudly. "Now, Dulcinea and two of her maids are riding on the finest steeds to greet you."

"Oh, Sancho, can it be true?" Don Quixote could hardly believe his ears. "You are not deceiving me?"

"I could never do that, Master," Sancho lied. "No, just ahead you will see two beautiful maidens riding on either side of the most beautiful of them all, Dulcinea of El Toboso."

Don Quixote excitedly followed Sancho down the road. After a moment, Sancho stopped and pointed to the three girls riding toward them.

"There she is, Master," Sancho said breathlessly. "Can you believe it?"

"Believe what?" Don Quixote asked with a puzzled look. "Did Dulcinea and her maids return to the city?"

"What are you talking about? They're right in front of you. Don't you see them?"

"Sancho, all I see are three peasant girls on

97

donkeys." Don Quixote was getting very annoyed. "Where is my Dulcinea and her maids?"

Sancho started to panic. Thinking fast, he put his hand over his mouth. "You think those are peasants? You really think your beloved Dulcinea looks like a peasant girl? I hope she didn't hear you."

Sancho got off Dapple and approached the girls. He dropped to his knees in front of the middle donkey.

"Oh, queen of beauty, princess of delight, it pleases me to introduce you to your humble servant, Don Quixote of La Mancha."

Don Quixote stood by Rozinante, dumbfounded.

"Get over here," Sancho whispered harshly. He pulled Don Quixote to his knees.

"Please excuse my master," Sancho said. "He is awestruck by your presence."

The girls looked at each other with disbelief. Don Quixote stared in puzzlement at the one in the middle. Her brown hair was pulled back behind her head, and freshly cut wheat clung to her long skirt. In the middle of her face, right between her mouth and her nose, was a huge brown mole.

"Hey, get out of our way," the middle girl demanded. "We got no time to waste with a couple of fools like you."

"Hear her sweet voice, Master," Sancho said to Don Quixote. Sancho turned back to the girl. "O wondrous Dulcinea, my master has come to offer his love and honor to the fairest maiden in the land."

Now the girl on the right spoke up. "Look, if you don't want your face rearranged, you'd better clear out," she snapped.

"Sancho, it is no use," Don Quixote said sadly. "An enchanter has beaten me here. He has turned my Dulcinea and her maids into these coarse peasant girls."

"Who are you calling coarse?" The middle girl rode by Don Quixote and kicked him flat on the ground. The other two girls rode after her, laughing scornfully at the disappointed knight and his squire.

"What have I done to deserve this?" Don Quixote wailed. "I cannot even see my Dulcinea's beauty. All I see is an ugly village girl."

"Oh, she wasn't so ugly," Sancho replied airily. "If you had used your imagination, Master, that mole above her lip would have disappeared."

"I am cursed, Sancho, cursed!" Don Quixote cried. "Who knows if I will ever see the Dulcinea I know and cherish?"

Sancho was relieved that his trick had worked. But he felt a little sad as he watched his beaten master drag himself back up on Rozinante and slowly ride away. Sancho just hoped he had done the right thing.

You know, I feel a little sad for Don Quixote too. To be so close to his beloved—or so he thought—and yet so far. This is almost worse for him than losing on the battlefield. Can Don Quixote continue his quest with the same courage and chivalry he had before?

16
Knight of the Lions

What can bring back the spirit of the old Don Quixote? Maybe a new adventure or fierce battle will do the trick. Don Quixote doesn't know it yet, but he's about to face the greatest test of his courage so far.

For the next few days, Don Quixote could do nothing but mope. Sancho tried to cheer him up.

"Master, you'll have other chances to see Dulcinea, I'm sure of it," the faithful squire said.

"Perhaps, Sancho, perhaps," Don Quixote said sadly. But he didn't sound as if he believed it.

"Now, listen here. Is it chivalrous for a knight to go around with such a long face?"

Sancho's words stung Don Quixote. "Sancho, you are bold to say such things—but you are right. It is not a knight's way to feel sorry for himself and carry on so."

"I didn't think so," Sancho said. "You're chasing a great dream—to fight the evils of the world and fill your life with adventure. Sometimes things are a little rough, but that's no reason to give up. So lighten up, Master. Things will get better."

Don Quixote felt better already. He felt better still when he saw a wagon approaching.

"Ah, Sancho, I think one of those adventures is at hand. A knight can smell the scent of excitement on the wind."

Sancho sniffed the air. "No, Master, that's not the scent of excitement. That's me. I forgot to take a bath this week."

"Look, up ahead," Don Quixote continued. "Here comes a wagon flying the flag of Spain. Who knows what it may bring us? Something to test my mettle, no doubt. **His mettle? Is that like steel armor or gold helmets? Not quite. This kind of mettle is a person's character, or inner strength. Just about everything in our story so far has tested Don Quixote's—and Sancho's—mettle.** Come, we shall ride to meet it."

Don Quixote set off at a gallop on Rozinante.

"Wait up, Master," Sancho yelled after him, digging his heels into Dapple's plump sides.

In a few moments, Sancho and Don Quixote were standing in front of a wagon pulled by a team of donkeys. Two men sat in the front. Don Quixote got off Rozinante and walked over to them.

"Where are you going, good fellows?" Don Quixote asked. "What are you carrying?"

The driver looked cautiously at Don Quixote. "It's my wagon. I'm bringing lions to the king. This man is their keeper." The second man nodded his head.

"Lions and a lionkeeper," Don Quixote said with

interest. "Is someone sending the beasts to the king's menagerie?" **A menagerie is a collection of animals. Years ago, many rulers and wealthy people kept animals in private zoos. Personally, I prefer to be kept in a comfortable chair.**

"Yes. A general found them in Africa and is giving them to His Majesty as a gift."

"Are these lions big?" Don Quixote wondered.

"Sir," the lionkeeper said, "they are the biggest lions I've ever seen. They're ferocious beasts, a male and a female, and each one is safely locked in its own cage."

"This is all very interesting, Master," Sancho said, impatiently. "But there's no adventure here."

"Not so fast, Sancho," Don Quixote replied. "I think an enchanter has created these lions to test me."

"Did you hear what the keeper said? A general is sending these lions—these huge lions—to the king. Nobody said anything about enchanters," Sancho insisted.

"Huge and *hungry* lions," the keeper added. "They haven't eaten all day."

"See," said Sancho, "you're asking for trouble if you tangle with these animals."

"Oh, Sancho, you worry so. I wager that these lions are no bigger than cubs," Don Quixote said.

"Yeah, cute little cubs with six-inch claws and big teeth. Leave them alone, Master," Sancho pleaded.

"Quiet, Squire. It is my duty to challenge these enchanted beasts. Keeper, please unlock the lions' cages," Don Quixote commanded.

"Your master is crazy," the keeper said to Sancho.

"No, he's not crazy," Sancho said, shaking his head, "just determined. Once he makes up his mind, there's no changing it."

The keeper turned back to Don Quixote. "These lions will rip you apart and probably do the same to the rest of us too."

Don Quixote drew his sword. "I can pin you to this wagon with my blade if you prefer," he threatened.

"Okay, okay, I get the point," the keeper said.

"Wait just a minute," the driver spoke up. "Let me untie my donkeys and get them out of the way before you open any cages. I don't want them turned into lion food too."

"Do what you must," Don Quixote said.

The driver took his donkeys to a tree and stayed with them, afraid to watch.

The keeper moved to the back of the wagon. "I'm doing this only because *he's* forcing me to. Anything that happens is his fault."

"Do not worry, lionkeeper," Don Quixote said. "I take full responsibility."

Sancho ran up to Don Quixote. Tears filled the squire's dark eyes. "Master, please, think about what you're doing. The windmill, the shepherds, even the Knight of the Mirrors—none of them was as terrible as this could be. I saw one of the lion's claws through the cage and it was b-i-i-ig. Sharp. Dangerous! This is no magic lion. This is the real thing!"

"It is your fear talking, Sancho," Don Quixote said. "I have no fear, so the beast does not seem so ferocious. Leave me to my duty, Sancho. If anything happens to me, you will head straight to Dulcinea and tell her of my fate. Now, say no more."

Sancho joined the driver behind the tree. The keeper neared the first cage at the back of the wagon. Slowly he opened the door of the cage which held the male lion. The keeper had not lied. The beast was enormous. The lion lay on the floor of the cage, its whiskers twitching. As Don Quixote approached, it turned its huge head and stared at the knight.

Wait a second. We're still basically talking about a cat, right?

"Come, lion," Don Quixote bravely called. "Let us each test our strength and courage."

The lion stretched to its full length and extended its front claws. The beast opened its massive jaws, its sharp teeth glistening...and yawned. Then the animal stuck out its tongue and leisurely washed dust from its face.

"Oh, so it's bath time, is it?" taunted Don Quixote. "Have you no stomach for my blade?"

Behind his tree, Sancho waited breathlessly to hear the sounds of battle.

"Hmm, no roaring lions. No screaming Don

Quixote. What kind of fight is this?" Sancho wondered aloud. He dared to peek between his fingers.

In the cage, the lion finished washing and stared again at Don Quixote. Then with a flick of its tail, the creature turned around and lay down for a nap.

"Keeper, take a stick and prod the animal," Don Quixote said. "He is slow to accept my call."

"Forget it," the keeper said. "Look, you challenged a huge lion. You're a brave knight, okay? Just be glad he didn't rip you to shreds, and call it a day."

Don Quixote weighed the keeper's words. "You are right. There is no disgrace for me if my rival refuses to do battle. Shut the door, and I'll signal to the others that all is well."

Don Quixote tied a white cloth to his lance and waved it in the air. Seeing the cloth, Sancho and the driver slowly made their way back to the wagon.

"You're alive!" Sancho shouted with relief. "Thank goodness, you're alive. Is the lion...dead?"

"No, it is sleeping peacefully in its cage. But the keeper will tell you that I bravely demanded a fight, and the lion had no taste for battle."

The keeper nodded and explained all that had happened. Sancho was impressed. His master was truly as brave as the knights in the books Don Quixote read. He swaggered over to the keeper and the driver.

"I told you guys my master could handle those lions," Sancho boasted. "You're looking at the greatest knight in all of Spain, maybe in all the world!" Sancho turned to Don Quixote. "I guess we'll have to give you a new name, Master. From now on, you should be known as the Knight of the Lions."

Don Quixote looked pleased. "Yes, it fits me well. Come, Sancho, our adventure here is over. Let us move on."

Boy, if that isn't every dog's dream—standing up to the biggest kitty on the block.

17
New Friends

Don Quixote—or I should say the Knight of the Lions—and Sancho Panza continued on their journey. They rode through thick forests and traveled along wide rivers. Finally, they came to a huge, green meadow. In the distance, Don Quixote spotted a small group of people on horseback.

"Master," Sancho Panza said, staring into the distance, "can you tell who those people on horseback might be?"

Don Quixote studied the group carefully before answering. "Judging by their fine dress and colorful banners, I would say it is some royal person on a hunt. Come, let us ride closer."

The two adventurers approached the hunting party. The woman leading the party was quite beautiful. She wore a hunting outfit that was even greener than the fields. Her straw-colored hair blew in the wind, and her laughter was like music on the wind.

"I believe it is a duchess, Sancho, a woman of noble birth. Ride over to her, and tell her that a great knight would like to meet her and offer his services."

"You got it, Master," Sancho quickly replied. He and Dapple set off toward the hunting party.

The Duchess watched Sancho bounce along on Dapple and stop in front of her. She smiled at the sight of the plump squire atop his equally plump donkey.

"Good lady," Sancho said with a bow, "my master, the brave knight Don Quixote of La Mancha, wishes to offer his services to your royal personage."

The Duchess smiled and nodded. "Well spoken, Squire. I have heard of this knight and his chivalrous deeds. Tell your master I would be honored to greet him and use his services."

Sancho bowed again, then turned toward Don Quixote. "Hey, Master!" he yelled. "She said it's okay for you to come over!"

Don Quixote cringed at his squire's yelling, but the Duchess only smiled at Sancho's simple ways.

Don Quixote rode up to the Duchess and introduced himself. Then he, Sancho, and the hunting party turned toward the Duchess's castle. At the gate, the Duke of the castle stood waiting to greet them.

"My lord," said the Duchess, "we are lucky to have a brave knight as our guest. This is Don Quixote of La Mancha and his faithful squire, Sancho Panza." She winked at her husband as if to share a private joke.

The Duke winked back. He and his wife had laughed over many tales of this strange knight. They had always thought it would be interesting to meet him and see if he was as amusing as they had heard.

Sancho got off Dapple to help his master dismount from Rozinante. But as Sancho swung his leg over the donkey's back, his foot got tangled in a rope hanging from his saddle bags.

"Whoa! Hold it—I mean, help!"

The squire dangled upside-down from the side of his donkey. But Don Quixote did not see his squire's mishap. He assumed Sancho was waiting by his side to help him off Rozinante. Without looking, Don Quixote quickly slid off his horse's back—and immediately tumbled to the ground. The Duke and Duchess tried not to laugh at their guests.

"Ah, brave knight, perhaps you could use some assistance," the Duchess offered.

"Yes, that might be a good thing," Don Quixote admitted humbly. "Perhaps a hand for my squire is in order too."

Two of the Duke's men picked up Don Quixote and untangled Sancho. Finally, everyone headed inside the castle.

This was a real castle, not an old, run-down inn such as the one Don Quixote had called a castle. Sancho's mouth fell open, and he stared in wonder. The palace had high stone walls, and the rooms seemed to stretch for hundreds of feet. Fine silks hung from the walls, and rugs from foreign lands covered the floors.

"Gentlemen," the Duchess said, "you must be tired from your travels. My servants will take you to your rooms and help you refresh yourselves. Then we will all meet for dinner."

Within an hour, Sancho and Don Quixote had bathed and rested, and they were ready for dinner with the Duke and Duchess. As they ate, the two guests talked about their many adventures. The stories of Don Quixote's bravery amused the royal couple, as did Sancho's loyalty to his master. The couple thought it would be fun to play along with their guests.

"Tell me, Sancho," the Duke said, "what do you hope to get out of all your adventures? I know your master wins glory for his Dulcinea and follows the code of chivalry. But what does a squire receive from such a noble quest?"

For once, Sancho was at a loss for words. "Well," he said slowly, "when we started, my master promised me an island. He said I could rule it any way I wanted. But I don't know if that's so important now."

"That's very wise, Squire," the Duke said. "Still, if you were promised an island, perhaps you should have one. I own a small island in the river nearby. I am willing to let you govern it for a time." **To govern is to be in charge. A governor is the fat cat who's in charge. Actually, governors are usually better when they're not cats.**

Sancho looked at Don Quixote. "I don't know, your highness. My master needs me, and I—"

Don Quixote interrupted him. "I will be fine here without you, Sancho. Our hosts' generosity will keep me in good spirits. This is your chance to fulfill *your* dream, Sancho! You should not refuse it."

"Yeah, but maybe it's not the best dream to have. You're the one who put the idea in my head. I never thought about ruling an island before. I'm happy doing what I do with you."

Don Quixote stood and put his hands on Sancho's shoulders. "I insist. You cannot refuse the Duke's offer. It has been your dream to rule!"

"Sancho," the Duke said, "our servants will prepare you for your trip to Barataria, for that is what the island is called. Go with them, and then sleep well. Being governor is hard work."

"That's what I'm afraid of," Sancho muttered as he shuffled off with the servants.

After Sancho left, Don Quixote turned to his hosts.

"You are most generous to give my squire this great opportunity. But it also saddens me to lose his companionship for even a short time. He is loyal, and he keeps me in good spirits. He is like no one else I know. At times, he believes nothing I say, yet he also believes everything I say. His trust in me is deep. I will miss him."

With that, Don Quixote excused himself from the table and went to his room. He would have a busy morning preparing Sancho for his own adventure.

Sancho has been a loyal squire. Now he's going to govern his own land. Is he prepared for this challenge?

18
Governor Sancho?

Before Sancho left for Barataria, Don Quixote offered his squire a few words of wisdom on how to be a good governor. For a guy with a very active imagination, the old "knight" had some very practical words for Sancho.

"Sancho, I have been thinking," Don Quixote said the next morning. "I feel I must say some important things before you go."

"You could say 'don't go,'" the squire said hopefully.

"No, no. What I want to say is this: Remember to be true to yourself. Know who you are and what is important to you. Take pride in your simple lifestyle, and don't let any man hold it against you."

"Yes, Master," the squire said, nodding.

"Next, always live a virtuous life. Do what is right. Others will respect your rule and follow your example."

"That sounds like a good idea," Sancho said, nodding thoughtfully. "Thank you."

"Also, as a ruler, you will have to make many important decisions. Always seek the truth in every instance, and don't let anyone try to sway your judgment with money."

"Right. I won't be tempted, even by bags of gold," the squire said. "Okay, that's good advice. Thanks, Don—"

"You should also take care to dress well, and keep your fingernails clean."

"My fingernails?" Sancho frowned. What did his fingernails have to do with being governor?

"And when you dine," Don Quixote continued, "never eat garlic or onions or other foods that will taint your breath with a foul smell."

"No garlic? But I love gar—"

"And finally, whatever you do," Don Quixote said solemnly, "do not eruct in public."

Sancho nodded. "No eructing." He paused. "Uh, Master, what exactly is eructing?"

"Belching or burping. Never, ever burp in public."

"Is that it? You're sure there's no more advice?" the squire asked impatiently.

"I believe that is enough, Sancho. Follow my advice, and your rule will always be remembered fondly on Barataria."

Finally, Sancho was ready to leave. The Duke's men took him and Dapple to a small boat, and they all set off down the river.

"Good-bye, Master! Good-bye, Duke and Duchess!" Sancho called. "Thank you again!"

"Good-bye, Sancho," everyone called back.

It took the boat only a few hours to reach the island. Barataria was not a large island, just a small town on some land in the middle of a river. Sancho carefully led Dapple ashore. He was greeted by an aide, who took Sancho to the center of town.

The people of Barataria came out to greet their new ruler. Many had been told of the Duke and Duchess's plan for Sancho. They rang bells and celebrated in the streets. "Hail to Sancho Panza!" they shouted.

"Hey, this isn't so bad after all," Sancho said. "I could get used to this."

But before Sancho even entered the governor's mansion, townspeople began coming up to him with their problems. As governor, Sancho was expected to settle all disputes.

"Nobody said there were going to be all these problems! Can't these guys settle things on their own?" Sancho asked his aide.

"But you are the governor, sir," the aide replied, trying not to laugh. "You are the one with the answers."

"Oh, yeah, I forgot. All right, let the people come."

The townspeople told Sancho their disputes over money and business deals turned bad. In each case, Sancho listened closely, then made his decision. For the most part, the Baratarians were impressed with his wisdom.

After he had settled all the problems, Sancho was led to a grand hall. Weapons and shiny suits of armor hung on the walls, and the town's most important citizens rose to greet their new governor. Four aides helped Sancho wash and took him to a banquet table.

"Ah, food!" Sancho said, rubbing his hands together. "This will be great. Bring me beef, lamb, veal, cakes. I want it all!" **Sounds like a meal fit for a king—or at least a governor. And I know a certain terrier who'd love to get at those bones when Sancho is done.**

As the groaning platter arrived, Sancho grabbed a leg of lamb. But before he could take one bite, a hand reached around him and snatched it away.

"Hey, what's going on?" Sancho demanded.

"I am sorry, sir, but this lamb may be spoiled. You might get sick if you eat it."

Sancho turned to look at the thief. "Who are you?"

"I am your personal doctor. It is my job to make sure you eat well and stay healthy." He chuckled to himself.

Sancho thought the doctor looked as if he had certainly eaten well—or at least often. His stomach bulged even more than Sancho's.

"Look, it's my first day on the job," Sancho pleaded with him. "Who's going to care if I get a little stomach ache?"

The doctor would not listen. He took away all the food, leaving Sancho with a few scraps of bread.

"This running your own island isn't all it's cracked up to be," Sancho thought. "What's going to happen next?"

Just then, Sancho's aide entered the room.

"Sir, a message has come from the Duke," he said importantly.

Sancho looked suspiciously at the aide. "What does it say?"

"The Duke warns that enemies may attack the island. You must be careful because there may be spies nearby."

"Enemies? Spies?" Sancho gulped.

"But do not worry. Come, you should rest now. You have much to do tomorrow," the aide said, hustling Sancho to his feet.

"'Don't worry,' he says," Sancho moaned. "'Rest,' he says. How? My brain is buzzing, my stomach is rumbling, and enemies I didn't even know I had want to attack me. And I've only been here for one day!"

Is Sancho in danger? Whom can he trust? And will the doctor ever let him eat a decent meal? This island is full of trickery.

During the next few weeks, Sancho forgot about enemies and spies. He was working too hard to worry. He had to make laws, give advice, and attend ceremonies. Being a governor, he discovered, was hard work.

Early one morning, Sancho heard soldiers shouting outside his room.

"To arms, to arms! The enemy approaches!" Soldiers burst through the doorway. "Sir, the battle is about to begin. You must lead us."

"Battle?" Sancho said, shaking with fright. "Shouldn't I stay here and command everyone? Isn't that what a governor does?"

The soldiers didn't listen to him. "Here is a shield, sir, and a lance," they said, shoving equipment into Sancho's hands. "You must lead us to victory."

A soldier strapped two shields on Sancho—one in front and one in back.

"I can't move. How do you expect me to—" Sancho waved one arm, lost his balance, and fell to the floor. He tried to roll to his feet, but he could only lie there helplessly, kicking his feet and waving his hands, like a turtle on its back. He closed his eyes and moaned as he heard more shouting and fighting around him. Sancho had never felt so ridiculous—or so helpless.

Suddenly, he heard a cry. "Victory! We have won!"

"Boy, I hope that was one of my soldiers," Sancho said. He opened his eyes and saw his soldiers dancing with joy.

"We won," Sancho shouted. Then everything went black. Sancho had passed out from relief. His men gathered around him and laughed.

"We shouldn't have done that," one soldier said.

"Oh, why not?" another replied. "I'm sure our governor likes a joke as well as anyone."

When Sancho finally awoke, he didn't wait for anyone to tell him the attack was all a joke. He went straight to the stable and found Dapple.

"Well, Dapple, I think I've learned something here. Being a governor is not what I'm cut out to do. I'm a simple man and a good squire. I don't belong here. I should be riding behind Don Quixote, helping him on his quest. I think it's time to leave."

Just then, Sancho's aide and the doctor ran out. They were astonished to see Sancho sitting on Dapple.

"Where are you going, sir?" the aide asked.

"Back to the Duke's castle, and Don Quixote," Sancho told him firmly.

"But sir, you rule us so wisely and so well," the doctor said.

"Yeah, sure. Thanks for the compliment, but I know where I belong. Good luck, and good-bye," Sancho called as he and Dapple headed down the road.

Within a day, Sancho was back at the Duke's castle. Don Quixote was delighted to see him.

"Sancho, my good squire, or should I say governor? What brings you back from your island?" Don Quixote asked.

"Forget being a governor," Sancho told him bluntly. "And it's not my island—I'm giving it back to the Duke. From now on, I'm going to leave the adventures to you. So, what have you been up to while I was away?"

"Ah, I missed you terribly, my friend," Don Quixote replied. "And, as before, I had to break the heart of fair maiden who fell in love with me. I explained that Dulcinea is the only woman in my life."

"Your devotion is amazing," Sancho said with respect.

"It is the chivalrous way," Don Quixote said humbly.

"Say, Master," Sancho said, "what happened to your nose?"

Don Quixote made a face and rubbed his hand over some red marks on his nose. "These wounds? I was attacked by a small enchanter with claws."

"Another enchanter?" Sancho looked closer at his master's nose. "They look like cat scratches to me."

"Yes, this enchanter did take the shape of a cat. He sneaked into my room and surprised me. But I drew my sword and chased him away. So, Sancho, are you ready to continue our journey? I have gone too long without performing knightly deeds and noble acts."

Good show, Don Quixote! We don't need any cats in this story, thank you.

"You bet!" Sancho said eagerly. This was the best news he'd heard all day!

Don Quixote and Sancho Panza thanked the Duke and Duchess for their generosity. Then they set off down the road to continue their noble quest.

Now the governor is just plain old Sancho Panza again, and he's a lot happier. But now his master is about to face his biggest battle of all.

19
Don Quixote's Last Battle

Have you ever heard of the word "quixotic"? If you look closely, you'll see it looks a lot like Don Quixote's name. That's because "quixotic" comes from "Quixote"! Quixotic (kwik-ZAH-tik) describes someone who's like Don Quixote (key-HO-tay): caught up with dreams of noble deeds and unreachable goals. A quixotic person is someone who bites off more than he or she can chew (a problem I never have). It goes without saying that Don Quixote is a very quixotic person.

D on Quixote and Sancho Panza left the castle and traveled along the coast of Spain. One day, Don Quixote was riding alone along the beach. In the distance, he saw a man on horseback riding toward him. Don Quixote realized it was another knight. The knight's armor covered him from head to toe, and his shield bore a painting of a white full moon.

"Greetings, illustrious knight," the man said to Don Quixote. "I am the Knight of the White Moon. I have ridden far to find you, Don Quixote of La Mancha, and challenge you to battle."

"Good knight," Don Quixote replied, "why do you seek to challenge me? I have done you no wrong."

"You insist that your maiden, Dulcinea of El Toboso, is the fairest in Spain. But I say it is my lady who is fairest. If you confess your lady is not the most beautiful, I will spare you. If you refuse, we must fight."

"Then we must fight," Don Quixote told him.

"If I win this battle," the knight said, "I will force you to swear Dulcinea is not the fairest maiden in Spain. You will also take off your armor, put away your sword, and return home. If you win, you can ask of me what you want."

"I agree to your terms, Sir Knight."

As the two knights prepared for battle, Sancho Panza came riding up on Dapple, followed by some people from the area.

"Not another joust," Sancho said to himself. To his master, he called, "Be careful, Don Quixote!"

The two knights rode away from each other, then turned at the same instant and began their charge. The Knight of the White Moon charged Don Quixote quickly. He didn't bother to use his lance. He just rode into Don Quixote so hard that both he and Rozinante tumbled to the ground. The knight scrambled off his horse and stood above Don Quixote, his sword drawn.

"Prepare to kill me, Knight of the White Moon. I still insist Dulcinea is the fairest maiden in all of Spain," Don Quixote said bravely.

"I will not kill you," the knight said. "I will not make you betray your chosen lady. All I ask is that you

do what you agreed: put away your armor, end your chivalrous quest, and return to La Mancha."

Don Quixote bowed his head. "I must keep my word. I will do as you say."

The Knight of the White Moon bowed to Don Quixote. Then he got on his horse and rode toward the town. Sancho ran to his master's side.

"Did I hear you right?" Sancho asked. "Are you really going to give up your quest?"

"You heard everything, good squire. I gave my word to accept his terms. I must return to La Mancha and put away my sword," said Don Quixote.

Sancho felt tears in his eyes. "Don Quixote, this is terrible. Being a knight is your whole life. Being a squire is my whole life. Sure, it had its ups and downs, but—"

"Sancho, I know your concern for me. But this is how it must be. I have fought to right wrongs and to help the innocent when I could. I have followed the code of chivalry. But now, sadly, it is over."

Meanwhile, at the other end of the beach, one of the local gentlemen ran over to the Knight of the White Moon. "Sir Knight," the man called, "I must know the name of the man who defeated the famous Don Quixote of La Mancha."

The knight stopped and pulled off his helmet.

"My name is Samson Carrasco. I was sent on a mission to send Don Quixote home. His friends and family think he is crazy. Months ago, I was supposed to defeat him in battle and force him home. But he beat me. I began to think like a real knight. I knew that I had to fight him again to defend my honor. Also, I had to do my duty. Now I have done both with dignity."

"You may think you are helping him," the local man said, "but this man you call crazy has lived honorably, always spoken the truth, and fought any evil he encountered. He has remained true to his chosen maiden, and he has never given up in his quest. Maybe we need more people who are as 'crazy' as he is."

Carrasco did not argue with the man. He simply turned his horse and rode toward La Mancha.

As Carrasco rode off, Sancho helped his master to his feet.

"Good friend," said Don Quixote, "perhaps it is right that we finally go home."

"How can you say that?" Sancho asked. He was upset. "Being a knight is such a noble thing to do."

"Yes, it is. I hope that when the record of my deeds is judged, I will be found to have done them honorably. I only failed in one thing: meeting my fair Dulcinea." Don Quixote sighed and closed his eyes.

"But all the people you sent to her must have told her of the things you've done. She must know all about the great Don Quixote by now," Sancho said. In that moment, Sancho forgot that Dulcinea was really the peasant girl, Aldonza. He had truly entered into his master's dream of chivalry and knighthood, and now Sancho did not want it to end.

"Perhaps, Sancho, perhaps," Don Quixote finally answered. "But I can't think of that any longer. I must return to La Mancha."

The two rode in silence for some time. Sancho hung his head as sadness overwhelmed him. But Don Quixote actually began to smile.

"Sancho," Don Quixote called. "I have an idea. When we get home, I will put away my armor as I promised. Then I will begin a simpler life. Sancho, my dream now is to become a shepherd."

Sancho thought a moment. "You know, that might not be a bad idea. I can't imagine sheep would try to knock us around or bounce us on blankets. Shepherds are good folk, noble in their way."

"Yes, it will be a good thing. We can tend our sheep by day and write poems and sing songs at night." Don Quixote was pleased with his new idea.

"Okay, Master, count me in. I want to be a shepherd too," Sancho said loyally.

Don Quixote and Sancho Panza sat up straight in their saddles. Now they had a new quest to keep their spirits high. The knight and his squire proudly rode home to La Mancha.

I feel a little sad about the end of Don Quixote's life as a knight. But just because one dream ended, Don Quixote didn't stop dreaming altogether—he found a new goal to pursue. He and Sancho know that Don Quixote was the best knight he could be. Maybe we do need a few "quixotic" people in this world. Sure, they may be dreamers, but their hearts are in the right place. And that's a wonderful thing.

Epilogue

Now we come to the epilogue, "So, what's an epilogue?" It's the last part of a book. In an epilogue, the author can explain what happens to the characters after the main action is over. Well, I have a little explaining to do about Don Quixote and Sancho Panza.

Don Quixote and Sancho did return to La Mancha. Don Quixote's niece and housekeeper were thrilled to see the knight arrive home safely. But they got a little worried when he said he wanted to become a shepherd. The niece thought her uncle was going crazy all over again!

But before Don Quixote and Sancho could head for the fields to tend sheep, Don Quixote became sick. He knew he was going to die. Before he did, he told all his friends and family that he had made a mistake.

"Sancho," Don Quixote said, "I was wrong to follow the foolish notions of chivalry in my books. I am no longer Don Quixote of La Mancha—I am just plain old Alonso Quixana again."

Sancho couldn't believe his master. He tried to convince the knight to keep his dream alive. But you have to remember that Cervantes, the author of *Don Quixote*, wanted to poke fun at the people who wrote and read books about knights. So even though he liked the character he created, Cervantes felt he had to say books about knights were silly. That's why he had Don Quixote renounce, or give up, his dream of chivalry.

Once he renounced his knighthood and his dream of glory, Alonso Quixana died peacefully in his house, with his faithful friend Sancho Panza by his side.

Now, the world is short one brave knight. But the need to dream and imagine never dies. You know, maybe I could be an imaginative knight and take Don Quixote's place. I could be Don Wishbono, defender of poor pups and enemy of evil cats—the bravest terrier in all of America. Saddle up my steed, good squire. The life of chivalry calls!